D0901665

THE GIRL IN THE MEADOW

British crime fiction at its best

JOHN DEAN

THE
BOOK
FOLKS

Published by The Book Folks

London, 2022

ISBN 978-1-80462-011-3

www.thebookfolks.com

THE GIRL IN THE MEADOW is the tenth book by John Dean to feature DCI Jack Harris. It can be enjoyed as a stand-alone or as part of the series. Details of the other books are available at the end of this one.

Chapter one

She lay where she had lain undisturbed for thirty years. Lying silently in the darkness, seemingly all but forgotten even by those closest to her and who loved her the most. Her life had been taken in a moment of wickedness that outraged all decency and she had been hidden away ever since where no one would look, out of sight, out of mind and rarely mentioned. However, the day was coming when she would be exposed to the light once more, when her memory could again be cherished and when dark secrets could at last be revealed.

* * *

Meadowview House had never seen anything like it in its one-hundred-and-sixty-three-year history as a steady stream of people made their way up the dirt track to its front door that bright autumn morning. Standing high on the slopes of a windblown North Pennines hillside, the house was used to being alone, having spent many decades serving as home only to the surly presence of George Stillwell, for whom visitors had been a rarity. George had sought out no one, no one had sought him out, and he had died alone and unmourned at the age of seventy-four. So solitary was his existence that his body was not discovered for six weeks following the heart attack that killed him in

1992 and even then only by accident, when a young hiker seeking directions knocked on the front door, became suspicious when it swung open and entered the house to find the old man lying in the kitchen. George Stillwell had died in the house where he was born and had spent his entire life.

Following his death, the house had stood alone for three further decades, its wallpaper peeling off, its paintwork flaking and its timbers rotting as it gradually sunk into dereliction. Its only company during that time, and even then only for a brief period following the old man's death, was a small group of teenage boys who viewed the empty house as a playground whose corrugated iron outhouses offered the ideal target practice for their airguns. When even they stopped coming after a few months, Meadowview House fell silent once more.

That had changed over the past year as life finally returned to the derelict property in the form of people who talked enthusiastically about refurbishing the building as they measured up and scribbled busily in their notebooks. Now, their work complete, they were ready to reveal full details of their plan and people had gathered in the chill of the bare-boarded living room, the musty air catching in the back of their throats as they waited for proceedings to begin.

Among those in attendance was a burly man, chisel-jawed and bright-eyed, who stood with two dogs at his feet, mongrels the both of them. For Detective Chief Inspector Jack Harris, the event was a welcome distraction from his daily duties as head of CID in the valley. He also had a strong connection with Meadowview House, stretching back to his years growing up in the area. Now, standing in the living room, memories of his teenage days came flooding back as he stared intently at the crudely scrawled piece of graffiti on one of the walls. The word was faded and difficult to decipher after all these years but still recognisable as "Hawk", the nickname that only those closest to him used.

The graffiti's survival brought to mind thoughts of simpler times, memories of the two teenagers who had been his closest friends before circumstances had driven them apart and forced the young Harris to leave behind his beloved valley. Now, three decades later, as he stood in Meadowview House once more, the detective saw again their faces and allowed their peals of laughter and the satisfying crack of airgun pellet on corrugated iron to echo down the years. He smelled once more the aroma of the cannabis that they had smoked. All of it was a reminder of days of innocence before the harsh reality of life brought their friendship to an end.

Harris could not know it in that moment, but they were events that were about to be played out once more.

A tall dark-haired man in his thirties noticed the detective's continuing perusal of the graffiti and walked over with a knowing smile on his face. The name tag on his lapel read "Ross Makin – Director, Three Valleys Wildlife Trust".

'I'm thinking of leaving it there and getting a blue plaque for it,' he said. 'Evidence of your nefarious activities as a teenager.'

'I'm not sure that anyone would be that interested,' replied Harris.

'You never know.' Makin nodded towards the graffiti. 'Anyway, enjoy it while you can, Jack, I've got the guys coming in first thing tomorrow to gut the place and it'll be lost for ever. Pity. I'd quite like to keep it as a way of thanking you for all the help you've given us.'

'I didn't do much.'

'You did enough,' said Makin. 'Your letter of support really impressed the National Lottery folks. Added to our credibility.'

'It's very kind of you to say so.'

Harris watched as more people entered the room, many of them heading for the display boards that bore artists' impressions of how the house would look when the renovation had been completed. He recognised several councillors and a couple of local businessmen. 'It's a decent turnout, mind, Ross. The great and the good.'

'Forget the great and good,' said Makin. 'The journalists are here, which is what really matters, and I noticed a local BBC film crew arriving just before I came in. A bit of telly will help us no end. We've got to remind people that this place still exists if the project is going to be a success.'

'It'll be a success and it'll give the media something positive to report on, for once.' Harris gestured to the graffiti. 'But I don't want you telling them that I did that. Or that I was one of those responsible for the holes caused by airgun pellets on the outhouses. I don't want the media delving into my past.'

'Don't worry. I won't.'

'Make sure you don't,' said Harris. 'That's the last thing I need.'

'You worry too much,' said Makin.

He patted the inspector on the shoulder and walked over to engage the councillors in conversation. Ten minutes later, with the BBC cameraman having set up his gear, Makin walked to the front of the room and stood next to the display boards. Silence settled on the room.

'Thank you for coming, ladies and gentlemen,' he said. 'I appreciate that it's a bit of a trek for you but, hopefully, it's given you a nice run out.'

Makin gestured towards a grainy black-and-white photograph pinned to one of the boards, depicting a man with unkempt greying hair and weather-beaten features who wore a tatty jacket and a flat cap and was leaning against a fence.

'We are here to pay tribute to George Stillwell,' he continued. 'Mind, I am not sure what he would have made of all this attention. George was not a man who readily embraced society. Indeed, this is the only picture we have of him. However, he is the reason we are here and we should all be grateful for the work that he did. Throughout the many years that he lived here, he devoted his life to preserving the wildflower meadows on the hillside behind the house with the result that they have survived as increasingly rare examples of a habitat that has been lost in so many other areas and which support abundant flora and fauna.'

Makin pointed to a series of photographs of wildflowers, beetles and butterflies that had been pinned to the board then tapped one of the artist's impressions of the renovated building.

'So, to the reason we have asked you here today,' he said. 'As you may recall from our announcement six months ago, the Three Valleys Wildlife Trust received approval from the National Lottery for funding to conduct a feasibility study on the renovation of the property. Today, I am delighted to announce that the Lottery has awarded us £1.5 million to carry out the full scheme, supplemented by a series of grants from several other organisations which bring the total to £2.4 million. This will allow us to press ahead with our plan to turn the house into a visitor centre and to ensure that we preserve the meadows for future generations.'

Murmurs of appreciation rippled round the room and there was a smattering of applause. Makin waited for the noise to die away before continuing.

'There are many people to thank for their support in making this happen,' he said. He gestured to a group of mainly young people standing in the corner of the room. 'Not least the Trust's team who helped to put together the bid for funding. I'd also like to thank the local council for their assistance and Detective Chief Inspector Jack Harris.'

Makin looked across to Harris.

'You probably know that, in addition to his duties running the local CID department, Jack is the force's wildlife liaison officer,' said Makin. 'He is also an acknowledged expert on the upland flora and fauna of the valley. Few people know these hills better and his support for our bid to the National Lottery was invaluable. Thank you, Jack.'

Harris inclined his head slightly.

'I am sure he would be happy to be interviewed afterwards,' added Makin.

The comment brought forth little reaction from the journalists; the detective's dislike for the media was legendary and they all had stories to tell of his reluctance to speak to reporters during investigations.

'So,' said Makin, working up to his conclusion, 'this project represents an exciting opportunity and...'

His voice tailed off as there was a commotion at the doorway and a man with grey streaks in his hair entered the room and pushed his way through the gathering until he reached the front where he jabbed a finger in the direction of the director.

'This is wrong!' he shouted. 'This house does not belong to the Wildlife Trust!'

Excited murmurs rippled round the room as the journalists sensed a story that was better than the one that had brought them to the house. They knew that their news editors would be more interested in a disturbance than they would be in butterflies and orchids. The journalists looked to Makin for a response. The director tried to appear calm, but everyone could tell that he was rattled by the intervention.

'We've been through this, Geoffrey,' he said wearily. 'We secured ownership of the house legally.'

'No, you didn't! It's mine! George Stillwell was my father.'

'You know as well as I do that there is nothing to connect you to this place,' said Makin.

'We'll see about that,' said the man.

He took another step towards Makin but Jack Harris moved swiftly to grab his arm.

'That will do,' said the inspector firmly. 'Unless you want to be arrested, that is.'

The man struggled but as the detective's grip tightened, he realised that resistance would be futile, nodded in defeat and became still.

'That's better,' said Harris. He slackened his hold. 'Now, whatever dispute you have with the Wildlife Trust, might I suggest that this is not the way to air it?'

'But,' said the man, and he pointed at Makin, '*he* won't listen.'

'Because it's not true,' said the director.

The man opened his mouth to retort but thought better of it when the inspector tightened his grip once more. He shrugged himself free and turned to go.

'You've not heard the last of this,' he said as he walked into the hallway, followed by the journalists. 'Not by a long chalk.'

Makin watched them go gloomily then noticed the expressions on the faces of the dignitaries, who had watched the altercation with mounting concern.

'He's just trying it on,' said Makin. 'There's nothing to substantiate his claim.'

The dignitaries relaxed a little and the tension eased. A few minutes later, with the sense of celebration punctured by the intervention, the proceedings broke up, people drifted away and Harris and Makin were left staring out of the living room window at the man as he gave interviews to the journalists on the unkempt front lawn.

'I was afraid this might happen,' said Makin gloomily. 'He's determined to ruin everything.'

'Who is he?'

'Calls himself Geoffrey Haynes. He turned up at the office a few weeks ago, demanding to see me. Claims to be the old man's son and that his real name is Stillwell. He's been making a pest of himself ever since.'

'But surely, you did all the checks when you bought the place?'

'You know we did. George died without making a will. A couple of heir-hunter law firms investigated the case – they even called in specialist genealogists – but he was an only child and they could find no record that he ever married or had kids. Every trail they followed ended up in a dead end, Jack. Take it from me, there are no living relatives.'

'That you know of.'

'This is all above board, Jack,' said Makin. 'Everyone had forgotten that the place even existed until I stumbled across it last year.'

'Has Haynes offered anything to support his claim?' asked Harris.

'He's got some cock and bull story about being taken to the house by his foster parents when he was a young lad, but he's produced nothing to back it up. If you ask me, he's nothing more than a con man who heard that we'd been awarded the money and decided to try to get some of it for himself.'

'It wouldn't be the first time that's happened. They're inveterate opportunists, are con artists. However…' The inspector's voice tailed off.

Makin gave him a sharp look.

'However?' he said.

Harris looked out of the window as the journalists concluded their interviews and Geoffrey posed for photographs.

'However,' said the inspector, 'in my experience, most con artists don't like giving interviews to the media – and they sure as hell hate having their picture taken.'

'Sounds like you think he could be telling the truth?' said Makin suspiciously.

'I'm just saying.' The inspector glanced towards the door as he heard the journalists re-entering the house, having concluded their interviews with Haynes. 'One thing's for sure, Ross. Those reporters are going to demand some answers and you need to kill this story PDQ before the funders change their mind. The last thing they'll want is to be dragged into a controversy.'

'But what do I say?'

'Tell them what you just told me,' said the inspector. 'That there's nothing to substantiate his claim. With any luck, they'll decide that it's not worth the risk running the story, although I wouldn't bet on it.'

'Will you talk to Haynes for me?' asked Makin as the journalists entered the room and headed towards them. 'See if you can't persuade him to stop this nonsense?'

Harris hesitated.

'Please,' said Makin. He gave the detective a beseeching look.

'Yes, alright. Do you know where he's from?'

'London.'

'Address?'

'I didn't ask,' said Makin. 'I had no intention of keeping in touch with him.'

'OK, I'll do what I can,' said Harris. He glanced at the approaching journalists. 'But don't say anything about my involvement to the media. This isn't an official enquiry. I'm only doing it as a favour to you.'

Makin gave him a grateful nod.

Harris brushed aside the journalists' questions and he and his dogs headed out into the bright sunshine. There the inspector saw a car heading down the track, moving at speed and too far away for him to read more than a partial registration number. Realising that once the journalists had finished with Makin, they would try again to extract a comment from him, the inspector gave a click of the tongue and the dogs followed him over to his white Land Rover. By the time the first reporter had emerged from the house, the inspector had long gone.

Chapter two

Jack Harris had a couple of calls to make on his way back to divisional headquarters so it was not until 2:00pm that he guided the Land Rover into the bustling hill town of Levton Bridge, whose properties clung to the side of the river that ran through the wooded valley. Halfway up the road leading to the marketplace, he pulled into one of the parking spaces in front of the Victorian building that housed the police station; the divisional commander disliked staff parking there so Harris did so whenever he could. Having got out of the vehicle and released the dogs, the inspector scowled as he saw a BBC reporter and cameraman emerge from the station and walk down the steps towards him.

'Would you care to make a statement about what happened at Meadowview House this morning?' asked the reporter. She held out her microphone and her colleague raised his camera to his shoulder.

'I have nothing to say,' replied Harris. He made to walk past them.

'But Ross Makin said you'd be happy to give us a quote.'

'About the plans for the visitor centre,' said Harris. He made as if to brush past her. 'Not what you want to talk about.'

'Oh, come on, Chief Inspector,' said the cameraman. 'Surely, you can tell us something? Geoffrey Haynes did commit a breach of the peace, didn't he? I mean, you had to intervene.'

Harris thought about ignoring the question but recalled the divisional commander's recent warning that he should be more co-operative with the media. 'At least try to look like you're trying to be helpful,' Philip Curtis had said following yet another complaint from a news organisation. So, now, the inspector looked into the camera.

'I can confirm that there was a minor incident during the launch of the project to transform Meadowview House,' he said blandly. 'However, no complaint has been submitted to the police so we do not propose to take any further action.'

'Will you be investigating Mr Haynes' claims that the house belongs to him?' asked the reporter.

'Whatever issue Mr Haynes has with the Three Valleys Wildlife Trust is a civil matter and, as such, has nothing to do with us.'

'So does that mean…?'

'I have nothing more to say,' replied Harris.

Brooking no further discussion, he strode up the steps, followed by the dogs. The cameraman watched the detective push his way through the front door of the police station and shook his head.

'So much for Jack Harris being happy to be interviewed,' he said.

'That was positively co-operative,' said the reporter. 'And it's still a decent story, whatever he says.'

'Maybe.'

'You're not sure?' asked the reporter.

The cameraman frowned.

'Ross Makin swears blind that there's nothing in it and that this Haynes fellow doesn't appear to have anything to back up his claim. In my experience, Ross is a pretty straight-up kind of guy. And now Jack Harris says that they're not investigating. Maybe Haynes is a crazy.'

'I still think there's a story in there somewhere,' said the reporter. 'And the Desk wants an updated package for the evening bulletin. Come on, there's not much more we can do here so let's get back.'

* * *

In the reception area, Harris was still scowling as he punched in the security code and passed through into the building proper. After climbing the stairs to the first floor, he and the dogs headed for the CID squad room where he found two of his team. Sitting at his desk was a balding man in a dark suit who was younger than Harris. He was talking to a matronly-looking woman, who was standing by the window that overlooked the front steps. After making a fuss of Scoot and Archie, Detective Inspector Gillian Roberts returned her attention to the BBC crew who were now loading their equipment into their vehicle. She looked over to Harris.

'I see the Beeb collared you,' she said. 'I take it you did as the commander requested and played nice with them?'

'I was my usual charming self.'

'Now that's where you go wrong,' said Detective Sergeant Matthew Gallagher. He winked at Roberts. 'Don't you reckon, ma'am?'

Roberts grinned.

'Sure do,' she said.

'It's always nice to receive the support of esteemed colleagues,' grunted Harris. However, the others could see that he was appreciating the banter. 'Anyway, there wasn't really much I could tell them. Either of you turned up anything on Haynes?'

'I did a quick search through the database,' said Roberts, 'but it's never heard of him. Nor Geoffrey Stillwell, for that matter.'

'I've come up blank as well,' said Gallagher. 'There's nothing on soft intelligence. If he is a con man, he's not using a known alias. The local telly ran a piece on the lunchtime bulletin, so I grabbed a still from the screen and circulated it round neighbouring forces in case anyone recognises him. You never know.'

'What about his car?' asked Harris. 'You turn up anything on that?'

'We narrowed it down to just the twelve hundred vehicles,' said Roberts. 'Nothing registered round here but plenty in London, which could be interesting if Ross Makin is right about him living there.'

'I put a call into a pal of mine in CID down there,' said Gallagher. A former Metropolitan Police officer, he had reluctantly moved north when his wife took a job as a nurse in the local hospital so that she could be nearer to her elderly parents. 'He's going to get back to me if they turn anything up.'

'We may get lucky, I suppose,' said Harris.

'So, can I assume that this is official now?' asked Roberts.

'Not yet,' said Harris. 'But it could yet turn out to be if the guy's a con man.'

Roberts and Gallagher exchanged glances.

'Out with it,' said Harris.

'Look, I know that Ross is a mate of yours,' said Gallagher. He was choosing his words carefully, so as not to irritate Harris. The sergeant had learned not to irritate his boss unless absolutely necessary. 'But wouldn't you expect him to say that the guy's a con man?'

'You don't believe him then?' said Harris.

'I'm not saying either way,' said Gallagher. He was relieved that Harris did not appear to object to the question. 'But isn't it possible that the Trust missed

Haynes when they did their due diligence and Ross is now trying to cover up for it? It would cause all sorts of damage to their reputation if he turns out to be genuine. Ross certainly came over as pretty defensive when the telly interviewed him.'

Gallagher waited for a negative reaction from the inspector, but it didn't come. Instead, Harris nodded.

'It's possible,' he said.

'So, what do we do now?' asked Roberts. 'We could end up wasting a lot of time on…'

She did not complete the sentence because a slim uniformed officer with thinning hair walked into the room. Divisional Commander Philip Curtis sat down at one of the desks and looked at Harris.

'The media seem to be getting pretty excited about this Haynes fellow, Jack,' said the commander. 'Is there anything in it?'

'Ross reckons he's trying it on,' said Harris. 'I said I'd have a chat with him on the QT.'

'Well keep it low-profile,' said the commander. 'You, of all people, know that the Meadowview House story is a big one for the area and I don't want us to do anything to ruin it unless we really have to.'

A female uniformed officer walked into the squad room.

'Sorry to interrupt,' she said. She looked at Harris. 'But that car you're looking for? The one belonging to Geoffrey Haynes? Well, one of our patrols has spotted it parked outside Liz Markham's B&B.'

'Excellent,' said Harris. He stood up. 'Fancy a walk, Matty lad?'

'Sure,' said Gallagher. He unhooked his jacket from the back of his chair. 'I'd quite like to meet him. The guy's got me intrigued.'

'Before you go,' said Curtis as the inspector headed for the door.

'You're going to mention the graffiti, aren't you?' said Harris. He turned back with a sigh.

'I am, yes. There was another incident last night. On the wall behind the Co-op and the parish council is distinctly unhappy at what it sees as our lack of enthusiasm for catching the culprit. Don't look like that, Jack. I need to be able to tell them something positive.'

'You can tell them that we're on it,' said Harris.

'That's what you said last time,' said Curtis, 'I mean, how difficult can it be to find a graffiti artist in a town this size?'

'I'm sure the team is doing everything it can,' said Harris. He glanced at Roberts, who nodded. 'They've carried out extensive enquiries.'

'And what exactly does that mean?' asked Curtis suspiciously.

Noting the inspector's irritation at the commander's comment, Gillian Roberts intervened to maintain the peace.

'I'll find out where we are with it, sir,' she said.

The commander nodded his thanks and Harris left the office, with Gallagher in tow. Curtis stood up and made to follow them.

'Stay!' said Harris's voice from the corridor.

The commander glanced at the dogs, who were heading for the door after their master then looked at Roberts.

'I'm never quite sure if he's talking to me or the dogs,' he said.

'I'm sure I wouldn't like to say, sir,' replied the detective inspector.

Chapter three

Harris and Gallagher arrived at the bed and breakfast five minutes after leaving the police station, having walked the short distance up the hill and into one of the side streets on the furthest side of the marketplace. On arrival, they confirmed with the owner that Geoffrey Haynes had booked in for an overnight stay and were led to a first-floor room. After the owner had gone back downstairs, Harris knocked loudly on the door but there was no answer. He tried again and, this time, Haynes did open the door and viewed the officers calmly as they held up their warrant cards. He stood aside to allow the detectives to enter the room.

'A chief inspector and a sergeant,' he said. 'I am honoured, indeed. Am I under arrest?'

'Should you be?' said Harris.

'Well, I've done nothing wrong.' Haynes closed the door so that their conversation could not be overheard from the landing. 'Not that Ross Makin would agree. I assume that he sent you to warn me off? Oh, don't look like that, Chief Inspector, I know what small towns are like.'

'Then you should know that nobody sends us anywhere,' said Harris. He always bridled at 'small town' insinuations when it was used to refer to the area for which he was responsible.

'Then what *do* you want?'

'We just want to get a better idea of what this morning was about,' said Harris. 'Clearly, you're upset.'

'Nobody else cares. Why should you be any different?'

'Because I don't appreciate people causing trouble on my patch,' said Harris. 'I could always charge you with wasting police time, you know. According to Ross Makin, you've produced absolutely nothing to back up your story.'

'That's because there isn't anything,' said Haynes. 'But I'm not making it up. George Stillwell *was* my father.'

'Then how come there are no official records to prove it?' asked Gallagher. 'A birth certificate, for instance?'

'I know what you're thinking. That I heard the Wildlife Trust had come into some money and saw a chance to cream some off for myself. Well, I'm sure that you've dealt with enough con men in your time and, if I was trying to scam the Wildlife Trust, don't you think I'd have put a bit more effort into it? Forged some documents, for example?'

'He's got a point,' said Gallagher.

'Maybe he has,' said the inspector. He looked at Haynes. 'Did George not leave you *anything* at all?'

'As far as I know, he never even acknowledged my existence.' Haynes' voice trembled slightly. It was the first time since they had entered the room that he had displayed emotion. 'He didn't want to know about his own son. Can you believe that?'

'What about your mother?' asked Gallagher. 'She must have cared about you?'

'I was told that she died giving birth to me. My childhood was spent moving from foster parents to foster parents. I never stayed anywhere for more than a few months.'

'You told Ross that it was a couple of your foster parents that took you to see the house,' said Harris. 'Is that true?'

'They shouldn't have done it, really, but they were soft and I kept badgering them to tell me who my parents were. Eventually, they said that my father lived in a house in the country. I think they only did it because they hoped I'd shut up about it.'

'But you didn't?' said Gallagher.

'I wanted to know the truth.'

'How come they took you to the house?' asked the sergeant.

'We came up here on holiday when I was five or six and the car stopped at the end of the track leading to Meadowview House, not that I knew it was called that at the time. My foster parents said that was where my father lived but that he was not allowed to see me and they were not allowed to tell me his name. When I tried to get out of the vehicle, they drove off. I cried for days afterwards.'

'So how come you didn't come back when you were a bit older?' asked Gallagher. 'I mean, why wait all these years?'

'Because I didn't know where it was. We lived in London and the north of England could just as easily have been Mars.' Haynes gave a slight smile. 'You are clearly from London, Sergeant. I'm sure you can appreciate that.'

Gallagher nodded; even though he had lived in the area for several years, he still did not feel at home in the valley. Too dark, too isolated and too quiet, he always said. Matthew Gallagher missed the bustle of life in the capital.

'Besides,' continued Haynes, 'a few days after we got back from holiday, I was sent to live with another couple. I think someone found out that my foster parents had broken the rules.'

'Did you not get in touch with them again when you were older?' asked Gallagher.

'I only knew them as Ken and Marion,' said Haynes. 'Besides, the foster care people told me that they'd moved house and that they couldn't tell me where they'd gone. London's a big city, especially when you're that age.'

'So how come you've turned up here all these years later?' asked Harris.

'Pure chance. I stumbled across a news story online about the plans for Meadowview House. I recognised it immediately.'

'And decided to hold a press conference of your own?' said Harris.

'I didn't plan to do it. The journalists caught me off-guard but, hopefully, it will have made Ross Makin take me seriously.'

'He's certainly done that,' said Harris. 'I have to say that it's a pretty flimsy story, though.'

'So, what do you suggest I do then?'

'Go home and forget all about it,' replied Harris.

Haynes gave a slight smile.

'I guessed that was why you were here,' he said. 'The law-abiding sheriff driving the troublemaker out of town. Perhaps you should be wearing a white hat.'

'I prefer to think of it as offering some friendly advice.'

'I'm sure you do,' said Haynes. He walked over to the door and opened it. 'Good day, gentlemen.'

A couple of minutes later, and after noting down Haynes' address and mobile phone number from the B&B's visitor book, the detectives headed back across the marketplace.

'So, what do you think, Matty lad?' asked Harris as they walked.

'It's either a desperately sad story or a highly inventive pack of lies,' said the sergeant. 'I'm tending to come down in favour of the pack of lies option. I can't see foster parents acting like that and I'm not sure a five-year-old would recognise a house that he had only glimpsed. No, I think Geoffrey Haynes is a con man. Perhaps we should go back and arrest him.'

'We'd be on somewhat shaky ground, I would suggest,' said Harris as they turned the corner, left the marketplace and started to walk down the hill towards the police station. 'We've nothing definite to say that it's a scam.'

* * *

Later that afternoon, the inspector was sitting in his office when the sergeant walked into the room.

'That London address that Haynes gave the B&B?' he said. 'It checks out. My mate popped round and asked the neighbours about him but no one had much to say. Keeps himself to himself, by the sound of it, and he hasn't been there for a few days.'

'Well, hopefully, he's got the message and that's the last we hear of him.'

'Hopefully,' said Gallagher.

Chapter four

The following morning, Meadowview House finally gave up the secret that it had guarded for thirty years. The grim evidence of the darkest moment in its history was uncovered when the workmen began to remove the floorboards in the living room, ahead of replacing the rotting timbers as the first stage of refurbishment of the building got under way. The two men worked steadily for the best part of an hour, with Radio 1 blaring out on the portable radio in the corner of the room as they loosened nails and prised open cracks, until one of them gave a cry and staggered backwards, his hand clapped to his mouth in horror.

'What's wrong?' asked his workmate, viewing him with alarm.

His friend did not reply but pointed to the floor with a trembling hand. Together, they stared down at the skull which surveyed them out of black holes where once had been eyes. Still recoiling with shock, the workmen ran out into the bright autumn sunshine where one of them crouched over and retched. He was still pale when the police patrol vehicle pulled up outside the house. The workman's colleague was little better and both men refused to accompany the two uniformed officers back into the house.

Having entered the property, the constables stood in the living room and looked down at the skeleton for a few moments before one of them glanced at his colleague.

'Are you going to tell Jack Harris, or should I?' he said.

The other officer gave him a rueful look.

'Rock, paper, scissors?' he asked.

* * *

While the uniformed officers were debating the point, the subject of their conversation was twenty miles away, sitting in his office at Levton Bridge Police Station with his mind occupied by more mundane matters. The dogs were curled up by the radiator in the corner of the room and, sitting uncomfortably on the other side of the desk, were the youngest detective constables on the inspector's team. Alison Butterfield, blonde and wearing her customary dark suit, was the senior of the two. Sally Orr, fresh-faced with short dark cropped hair and wearing a blue pullover and black trousers, was younger and the newest recruit to plainclothes work. Both were eager to make their mark but were finding that their enquiry into the graffiti incidents in the town was offering little opportunity to please their boss.

'I still can't believe that we don't know who's behind this,' said Harris. He shook his head. 'Surely, we must have some idea? It's a small enough town, for goodness sake.'

'We think it's a kid,' said Butterfield. 'Someone who thinks they're the next Banksy.'

'It doesn't take a genius to work that out,' said Harris. 'Have you gone down to the comprehensive at Roxham? Surely, someone there recognises the tag? Boz must be someone's nickname.'

'If they do, no one is saying,' said Butterfield. She was cursing herself for the off-hand tone of her previous answer and tried hard to sound more professional. 'And we've made extensive inquiries.'

'Don't kid a kidder, Alison,' said Harris. 'Extensive inquiries is what I tell Curtis when I'm not taking something as seriously as he would like.'

'But we have been taking it seriously,' protested Butterfield. 'For instance, we checked with the hardware store in the marketplace but only one person has bought spray paint over the past month and that was the vicar at St Joseph's. He bumped his car into a traffic bollard last week, remember?'

'So, he did,' said Harris. He chuckled. 'Who would think that a man of the cloth could use such profane language? Fair tests your faith, it does.'

The comment eased the tension felt by the young constables and they allowed themselves to smile. As was often the case with his younger officers, Harris's irritation had dissipated as quickly as it had flared up.

'Look,' said the inspector, trying to sound more conciliatory. 'I know I'm giving you a hard time about this, but the parish council chairman has been bending Curtis's ear about it, Curtis has been bending my ear and now I'm bending–'

He did not finish the sentence because his desk phone rang and he picked up the receiver. His eyes widened as he listened to the voice on the other end for a few moments.

'I'm on my way,' he said. 'You know the drill. Make sure that the workman don't touch anything and that no one goes into the house until I get there.'

Harris replaced the receiver and looked across the desk at the constables.

'It looks like I've got something a bit more exciting than catching young Boz,' he said. The inspector lifted the receiver again and punched in the internal number for the detective inspector's office. 'Gillian. I've just had one of the uniform lads on. A skeleton has been found by workmen at Meadowview House. Can you contact the usual people, please? Oh, and if Matty's there, can you ask him to meet me round the front?'

'Will do,' said Gillian Roberts. 'We should check if Geoffrey Haynes is still in town. It's one heck of a coincidence that he should turn up just as the body was likely to be found.'

'I'll get Alison and Sally to run over to the B&B.' Harris replaced the receiver, stood up and looked at the constables. 'You get the gist of that? I want to know if Haynes did leave, as he promised.'

They nodded and their eyes gleamed with excitement; this was more like it, they thought.

'What do you want us to do if he is there?' asked Butterfield. 'Arrest him?'

'Only if he resists,' said Harris. He walked over to a peg on the wall and removed his jacket. 'I want this kept low-profile until we know what we're dealing with.'

* * *

An hour and a half later, Harris was back at Meadowview House, a double-fronted, two-storey red brick property that stood in the middle of a garden populated with overgrown shrubs and windblown apple trees. The inspector was standing in the dark and musty living room, one wall of which was lined with empty bookshelves. There was also an old fireplace that still bore the remnants of its last blaze many decades before. Harris stood and watched as a white-haired man crouched down to peer closely at the skeleton, which was now fully revealed following the removal of more floorboards. Like the forensics officers who had begun their painstaking examination of the room, Home Office pathologist Professor James Rokeby was wearing white overalls, as were Harris and Gallagher.

'Well, Doc?' said Harris. 'What can you tell us?'

'Not a lot for definite, at this stage,' said the pathologist. He straightened up, winced at the pain from his arthritic knee and gave the inspector a grateful look as Harris handed him his walking stick. 'And anything I can tell you will be mostly guesswork until I can do a more thorough examination of her.'

'Anything will do at this stage.'

Harris noticed that Gallagher was studying the name "Hawk" scrawled on the wall.

'No wonder we've not caught Boz,' said the sergeant, with a slight smile. 'You and he are clearly part of the same massif. I take it that *this* is your handiwork?'

'I am afraid so,' said Harris ruefully. 'Evidence of my misspent youth.'

'And a lot of it was misspent,' said the pathologist. He gave the inspector a mischievous look. 'Although perhaps I shouldn't embarrass you in front of your junior officer.'

'Matty knows that I was no angel.' Harris switched his attention back to the skeleton. 'So, it's a woman then?'

'Yes. Late teens, early twenties, at a guess. And blonde. There are strands of hair. I think that she was left here relatively recently.'

'How recent?' asked Harris.

'Recent in these terms could be anything over the past few decades,' said the pathologist. 'Thirty, forty years, maybe, could be more, could be less. I should be able to say more after the post-mortem.'

'Will you able to say if she was placed here before or after the old man died?' asked Gallagher.

'I'm not sure I'll be able to be that precise, even after the examination. However, an old pal of mine is a forensic archaeologist in Newcastle. I'll give him a ring and see if he can help me out. If anyone can answer your question, he should be able to.'

Gallagher stared back at the graffiti and frowned.

'Something wrong, Matty lad?' asked Harris.

'It's not beyond the bounds of possibility that the body was here when you and your mates came to play with your airguns, is it?' said the sergeant. He was selecting his words carefully. 'And she would have been of a similar age.'

Harris gave him a sharp look.

'If you're suggesting that we had—' he began.

'I'm not suggesting anything,' said Gallagher. 'But it complicates things, does it not? You know what the Brass are like about conflicts of interest. I mean, you're going to have to tell Curtis, aren't you? And he's bound to tell the high-ups.'

'We'll cross that bridge when we come to it.'

'Yes, but you can't keep it—'

'There's no point worrying about it now,' said Harris. His voice brooked no dissent. 'We've got plenty of other things to think about.'

Gallagher surveyed the resolute expression on the inspector's face then glanced at Professor Rokeby, who held up his hands.

'Don't involve me in this, Matthew,' he said. 'This is between you and your governor.'

'Well, I've said what I have to,' said Gallagher.

'You have and it's duly noted.' Harris looked back to the pathologist. 'Anything to identify her, Doc?'

'There's no ID and experience tells me that we could struggle with someone who's been there that long. Hopefully, we can get an ID on dental records.'

'What about DNA?' asked Gallagher.

'We'll be able to take a sample but the problem will be matching it,' said the pathologist. 'DNA profiling was still in its infancy then, remember. It's taken a long time to build up a database and I'd bet my last dollar that our Jane Doe is not on it. There might be a link with someone on our more recent records, I suppose.'

'Sounds like a long shot,' said the sergeant.

'I am afraid so. And one that will take time.'

'Maybe she's connected to Geoffrey Haynes,' said Gallagher. He looked at Harris. 'Maybe it's his mother. He said that she died giving birth to him, didn't he? Maybe our suspicions were right and he does know about the body. Any way you can tell if she's had a baby, Doc?'

'Not until I conduct a more thorough examination. She's certainly old enough.'

'Any idea how she died?' asked Harris.

'Nothing obvious.'

'So Matty could be right?' said Harris. 'She died during childbirth?'

'It could be natural causes, I suppose,' said the pathologist. 'But until we know better, might I suggest that you treat her death as suspicious? After all, dead people tend not to hide themselves under floorboards, do they?'

'Particularly not if they're a dirty secret,' said Harris.

There was a knock on the window and the detectives turned to see Ross Makin gesturing to the inspector. The detectives went outside where the director nodded towards the two workmen, who were standing nearby talking to a couple of uniformed officers.

'I've given them the rest of the day off,' said Makin. 'But I need to know if they can start work again tomorrow? They're not going back in if the skeleton is still there but I'm assuming that you'll take it away today?'

'We will,' said Harris. 'But our forensics people will probably be here tomorrow as well. And if it turns out to be a murder, that would make it a crime scene and your guys will not be back in for a long time. Weeks, possibly months.'

'Months?' exclaimed Makin. 'But we plan to open the visitor centre on 23 March.'

'Well, you may have to put it back.'

'And I thought you were on our side,' said Makin churlishly.

'It's not a case of sides, Ross. It's the law.' Harris tried to look encouraging. 'Look, if it turns out to be natural causes, you could be back in a few days.'

'And if it's not?'

'Then Meadowview House is mine until I say otherwise.'

Like it was once before, thought Gallagher but did not voice the thought. Before Makin could protest further, a car headed up the drive towards the house. When it drew to a halt, Butterfield and Orr got out.

'No luck at the B&B then?' said Harris.

Butterfield glanced at Makin.

'You can talk in front of Ross,' said the inspector.

'Haynes left an hour after you and the sarge went to see him,' said Butterfield.

'Surely, you don't think this is anything to do with him?' said Makin.

'To be honest, Ross, I don't know what to think,' said Harris.

Makin buried his head in his hands.

'This is a nightmare,' he groaned.

'Welcome to our world,' replied the inspector.

Chapter five

The next morning, with the dogs trotting obediently at his heels, Jack Harris was approaching the first-floor briefing room at Levton Bridge Police Station for an 8:00am catch-up with members of his team when Philip Curtis walked towards him.

'Just the person,' said the commander. His face bore a stern expression. 'You and I need to have a talk.'

'If you're going to ask me about our graffiti artist, I haven't had a chance to–'

'It's something much more serious than that,' said Curtis. 'About our Jane Doe.'

'Can't it wait until I've talked to the guys?' said Harris. 'I should know more then.'

He made as if to continue his walk to the briefing room. The commander's expression had led him to guess what was coming and Harris had no desire to discuss it with Curtis; in the inspector's view, his private life was just that, a private matter. He was not surprised that word about it had already reached the commander and the inspector silently cursed Gallagher.

'In my office,' said Curtis. 'Now.'

Harris held up his hands in mock surrender and followed the commander along the corridor. Once they were in the room, Curtis sat down behind his desk and gave the inspector a hard look. Harris knew it was serious because the commander did not even object to the presence of the dogs in the room; it was the first time they had been allowed in his office.

'Shut the door, please,' said Curtis.

Harris did as he was instructed and sat down on the other side of the desk.

'What's the problem?' he asked. He had decided to play the innocent. It didn't work.

'You tell me. I appear to be the only person who did not know about your connection to the body in Meadowview House.' The commander's frustration had turned to a sense of hurt. 'I know we have different approaches to the job, but I really thought that we had developed an effective working relationship since I arrived here. Certainly not one in which we keep things from each other.'

'I haven't kept anything from you.'

'Don't play me for a fool!' exclaimed Curtis. 'Is it true that you played in Meadowview House as a teenager?'

'I take it that Matty Gallagher has been letting his mouth go?'

'He didn't need to. It's the talk of the station. What's important here is not who told me but why I am the last person to hear about it and then only via water cooler gossip?'

'I didn't mention it because it's not relevant,' said Harris.

'Not relevant that my detective chief inspector could have been feet away from a dead body buried under the floorboards?' exclaimed Curtis. He shook his head in disbelief. 'Give me some credit, Jack!'

Harris sensed that the time had come for a more conciliatory approach.

'OK, OK,' he said. 'Maybe I should have told you.'

'There's no maybe about it,' said the commander. 'This has put me in a very difficult position, Jack. It makes me look as if I am not in control of my own police station.'

'In my defence, for all we know, the Jane Doe was placed there long after I played there with my mates. Or long before. Whenever it happened, it's got nothing to do with me because neither me nor my pals knew anything about it and I don't like my private life being the subject of idle gossip.'

'It's too late for that,' said Curtis. 'What were you doing at the house anyway?'

'I've never made a secret of the fact that, as a teenager growing up round here, I fell in with a bad lot. Well, after Old Man Stillwell died, some of us heard that Meadowview House was empty so we used it as a hideaway from the police.'

'And what exactly were you doing that you didn't want the police to know about?' asked the commander. 'Or don't I want to know?'

'Just hanging out. Smoking weed and firing airguns at the outhouses. The usual things that teenagers do.'

'I didn't do anything like that,' said Curtis.

Harris gave a slight smile.

'No, I don't suppose you did,' he said. 'And, for the record, events in my past have never stopped me doing my job. You know that.'

'I do, yes,' said Curtis. 'And headquarters agree.'

'You told them?' Harris frowned. 'Why on earth would you do that?'

'I had no alternative. They needed to know and, for the moment, they're fine with you running the investigation. However, I don't need to tell you that there're some folks will use it against you. Take this as a friendly marking of your card, Jack. Understand?'

'Understood,' said Harris.

He stood up and headed for the door, followed by the dogs.

'Before you go,' said Curtis. '*Is* there any news on the graffiti artist? The council chairman and clerk are coming to see me this afternoon and I promised them an update.'

'We're making extensive enquiries.'

'Don't think I don't know what it means when you say that.'

Harris gave the commander a bleak look and left the room. Once outside, he muttered a curse under his breath.

'I heard that,' said Curtis's voice from the office.

Harris sighed and headed for the briefing room where he found Roberts, Gallagher, Butterfield and Orr, and Detective Constable Alistair Marshall, a slim dark-haired man in his twenties. They were sitting around a large table, each one of them uncomfortably aware that they had little to tell their boss. Their mood was little improved by the inspector's thunderous demeanour.

'So,' said Harris as he sat down. 'Who's been gossiping about me behind my back?'

The detectives looked confused.

'Don't give me the innocent,' said Harris. 'Someone has been telling Curtis about me playing at Meadowview House when I was a teenager. Matty lad, anything to say?'

'It wasn't me,' protested Gallagher.

'Well, it's a hell of a coincidence that you and I talked about it yesterday and now it's all over the station.'

'I didn't tell Curtis,' repeated Gallagher. He noted that Harris still looked unconvinced. 'I'm sure that none of us would go behind your back.'

Everyone murmured their agreement.

'Well, *someone* is stirring things up,' said Harris. 'Anyway, what have we come up with about events at Meadowview House?'

'Precious little,' admitted Roberts. 'We haven't been able to find anyone who was close to George Stillwell. His only regular visitor seems to have been the postman, and the only other people he saw often were the ladies in the village shop in Ellerby and, even then, he didn't talk much.'

Harris glanced at the wall clock.

'The Press Office is about to issue an appeal for information,' he said. 'Maybe that will bring forth something. However, we should not have to rely on the media. Surely, we've been able to turn up something ourselves?'

'You always say that everyone knows everyone's business in the valley,' said Butterfield. 'But, with all due respect, guv, you're wrong when it comes to George Stillwell.'

Gallagher rolled his eyes in exasperation and the young detective constable immediately regretted her comment. Gallagher was continually cautioning her to hold her tongue lest it run away with her but before Harris could offer a retort, Gillian Roberts hurriedly intervened.

'She's got a point, Jack,' she said. 'The man was practically a hermit.'

Harris nodded.

'Aye, maybe you're right,' he said. 'But I still need something to tell the reporters. Once the news gets out, the Press Office phone won't stop ringing. What about Forensics? Anything from fingerprints?'

'Every stick of furniture from the house ended up in a skip when the Trust took the house over,' said Gallagher. 'Forensics say that what few prints remain is a real jumble.'

'So, what about the law firms that tried to track down relatives after George died?' asked Harris. 'Is there a chance that they missed Geoffrey Haynes?'

'There were two companies,' said Butterfield. Relieved that her earlier comment had not earned her a reprimand, the constable was keen to sound as if she had been doing something useful. 'One ceased trading years ago and the other one has been merged three times and they're not sure that they still have the research.'

Harris shook his head but, before he could reply, his mobile phone rang. He took the call and listened for a few moments then grunted and placed the device back on the table.

'Another dead end,' he said. 'Doc says that our Jane Doe had not given birth so there's no way that she was Haynes' mother.'

'Maybe she was his sister,' said Gallagher. 'The dates could still fit, couldn't they? If Haynes thought that she would inherit a share of the house, that's a motive for murder.'

'What, George Stillwell goes from lonely old hermit to full-blown family man?' Harris shook his head. 'Sorry, Matty lad, but I'm not sure I buy that.'

Harris looked at Gillian Roberts.

'Any luck on missing person reports for young women?' he asked.

'I am afraid not,' said Roberts. 'It was a largely paper-based system in those days so even if we could narrow down the dates, God knows how we track down the right report. When it comes to cold cases, this one is as cold as it gets.'

Silence settled on the room as Harris digested all he had been told. The silence was broken by a knock on the door as one of the reception staff walked in.

'Sorry to interrupt, sir,' she said, looking at Harris. 'But Geoffrey Haynes has just come into the front office with his solicitor. Says he wants to report a crime.'

'Not the murder of his sister, by any chance?' asked the inspector.

'He wouldn't say what it was about, sir. Said he'd only tell you.'

'OK,' said Harris. He stood up. 'Care to join me, Matty lad? Maybe this case isn't so cold, after all.'

Once they had gone, Butterfield grabbed her coat and headed for the door as well.

'I'm off to check out a couple more people who might have known George Stillwell,' she said. 'You fancy coming, Alistair?'

'Sure,' said Marshall and followed her out of the room.

'Let me know if you find anything useful!' Roberts shouted after them. The words 'will do' drifted back from the corridor. The detective inspector stood up and looked over to where Orr was sitting. 'You going to be in for a while, Sal?'

'Yes, ma'am. I've got some calls to make.'

Roberts nodded towards the dogs, who were curled up in their customary position by the radiator in the corner of the room.

'Will you keep an eye on the boys until Jack gets back then?' she asked.

'Sure,' said Orr. The constable frowned.

'Something bothering you?' asked Roberts.

'Could this thing about the governor playing at Meadowview House be serious?' asked the constable. 'I thought it was just idle gossip at first, but it sounds more than that.'

'It could be,' said Roberts. She gave Orr a sharp look. 'I hope that you're not the one who's been talking about it.'

'No, of course not,' said the constable quickly. 'I just wondered.'

'I guess it helps to know about these things,' said Roberts. She walked over to close the door and returned to her seat. 'Stops you saying the wrong thing to the wrong person. You'll be aware that, when he was a teenager, Jack left the valley to join the Army to stop himself getting in trouble with the police? And that when he came out, he joined Greater Manchester Police where he had such a meteoric rise that he was appointed to head the new gangs unit?'

Orr nodded.

'Well not everyone welcomed the news when he came back here,' said Roberts. 'Some officers were jealous of his reputation and resented the fact that he'd got the job over them so they started saying that the post should not have gone to someone who counted among his former friends, men who ended up as career criminals. This Meadowview House is manna from heaven for them.'

'But aren't we all on the same side?' said Orr.

Roberts gave a slight smile.

'Ah, the naivety of youth,' she said.

Chapter six

Harris and Gallagher sat in the interview room and looked across the table at Geoffrey Haynes and his lawyer, a thin, balding man whom neither detective recognised. Gerald Lucas was not based in the valley and neither officer had heard the name before, which added to the sense of intrigue. Harris switched his attention to Haynes, who was sitting with his arms crossed. The detective recognised the same confidence that Haynes had exhibited at Meadowview House the first time they had met. Haynes conveyed the impression of a man who felt in control of the situation and Harris, who had always prided himself on being the one in charge, glanced at Gallagher, who raised an eyebrow.

'I understand you wish to report a crime?' said Harris.

'I do, yes,' replied Haynes.

'Then I have to inform you that anything you say will be—'

'I don't think that is really necessary, do you, Chief Inspector?' said Gerald Lucas. 'My client is here as a victim, not a suspect.'

'A victim?'

'What else would he be?' asked the solicitor. 'He wishes you to investigate a crime committed against him. The theft of Meadowview House by the Three Valleys Wildlife Trust.'

'Yes,' said Haynes. He nodded vigorously. 'That house belongs to me and they took it. I want them prosecuted.'

'We've gone through this already,' said Harris. He decided to hold back the information about the skeleton for a moment or two; he wanted to gauge Haynes' reaction when he was told about the find. 'You've got nothing to prove your claim. You admitted as much.'

'Yes, but if I report a crime you have to investigate it, don't you?'

'Not if we think that you are wasting police time, we don't. You can be charged for that. The courts take a very dim view of it.' Harris looked at the solicitor. 'Surely, you've made it clear to him that he does not have a case? How come you've allowed yourself to be roped into this nonsense, anyway?'

'Mr Haynes came to our office in Carlisle yesterday afternoon and retained our services to act for him in this matter,' said Lucas.

'And did he show you any proof that the house belongs to him?' asked Harris.

'Well, no, he didn't, but he is adamant that the validity of his claim can be proved in a court of law.'

'Civil law, maybe,' said Harris.

'I beg to disagree,' said the lawyer. 'Like my client says…'

Sensing that the conversation was about to go round in circles, Harris decided that the time had come to reveal the discovery of the skeleton.

'So, he knows nothing about the body then?' he said in a matter-of-fact way.

Haynes and the solicitor looked startled. It seemed to both detectives that the reaction was genuine.

'What body?' asked the lawyer.

'The human remains that were found concealed beneath the floorboards at Meadowview House yesterday,' said Harris. 'A young woman.'

The lawyer gave Haynes a questioning look.

'Did you know about this?' he asked.

'Of course I didn't,' said Haynes but he appeared to have been shaken by the revelation.

'Nevertheless,' said Harris, 'it is a remarkable coincidence that you should turn up just as it was likely that the remains would be found. It certainly got us thinking, didn't it, Sergeant?'

'It certainly did,' said Gallagher. 'First rule of murder investigation – there's no such thing as coincidence.'

'Murder?' said Haynes. He had gone pale and looked uneasily at the detectives; his confident demeanour of a few moments previously had been replaced by something much less bullish. 'What do you mean, murder?'

'Cause of death has not been confirmed yet,' said the inspector. 'But we are treating it as suspicious. Bodies don't get under floorboards on their own.'

'Well, I know nothing about this,' said Haynes. His confidence was returning. 'And you have nothing to prove otherwise.'

'Be that as it may, it does change things, does it not? For a start, I assume that you will wish to abandon your claim about ownership of the house?'

'Why would I do that?'

'Because as it stands, you are very definitely a person of interest to us. After all, someone put that body there.'

'Now hang on a min–'

'Listen, Mr Haynes,' said Harris. 'I'm giving you the opportunity to stop wasting everyone's time. You picked the wrong house for your scam. Admit that you made it all up and you can walk away without any further action being taken against you.'

'It's not a scam!' protested Haynes. He turned to his solicitor for support. 'Tell them.'

'Perhaps if we could know the young woman's name, it might help,' said Lucas.

'We were hoping that your client may be able to tell us that,' said the inspector. 'We are wondering if it might be a relative. Someone with an equal claim to ownership? His sister, perhaps?'

'That house is mine and mine alone!' exclaimed Haynes.

'It would be if someone had murdered your sister,' said Gallagher.

'This is preposterous!' exclaimed Haynes. He stood up. 'And I am not going to stay to listen to such rubbish.'

'Sit down!' said Harris.

Haynes hesitated, noted the stern expression on the detective's face and glanced at his solicitor, who nodded. Reluctantly, Haynes sat down.

'There is one way to resolve things,' said Harris. 'A DNA sample, which would prove if there is a familial link between the two of you.'

'Of course there won't be,' said Haynes.

'Then might I suggest that you agree to the chief inspector's suggestion?' said the solicitor. 'I mean, it does seem reasonable.'

Haynes did not reply.

'Would you allow me a few moments with my client?' asked the solicitor. 'In private?'

'Surely,' said Harris.

Once the detectives were back in the reception area, Harris looked at his sergeant.

'I'm sorry I had a go at you earlier, Matty lad,' he said. 'I was hacked off that someone is trying to make trouble for me. I should have known that you would not go behind my back.'

'None of us would.' Gallagher looked both ways along the corridor and lowered his voice. 'Look, I didn't want to say anything in the briefing room but, from what I'm hearing, it could well be Alan Jay who's stirring things up.'

'That would be my guess,' said Harris. 'He's a vengeful bastard and he's not forgiven me for getting this job ahead of him.'

'Not to mention that he blames you for getting him moved back into uniform and sent to drive a desk at headquarters,' said Gallagher. 'He thinks it was you who suggested that he become head of the Administration Unit. Apparently, you said that someone needed to count the paper clips.'

'Too subtle for the likes of me,' said Harris. However, his slight smile suggested otherwise. 'But he's waiting for an opportunity to undermine me and this is it, particularly since he's got his eye on taking over as head of the Professional Standards Unit when Maeve Riley retires.'

'But who told him about your link to the body?' asked Gallagher.

'There were plenty of uniformed officers and forensics people at the house. Folks gossip, don't they?'

Gallagher shook his head.

'Office politics,' he said. 'Don't you just love it?'

'Not really,' said Harris. He looked back towards the interview room. 'What do you make of Haynes then?'

'He looked genuinely surprised when you told him about the body and it doesn't sound like he's going to drop his claim that the house is his.'

'It's catch-22, Matty lad. If he admits that it's a scam, we can charge him with attempted fraud, and if he sticks with his claim that the house is his, that makes him our number one suspect in what could turn out to be a murder inquiry.'

'Damned if he does, damned if he doesn't,' said Gallagher.

'Exactly.'

The door to the interview room opened and the solicitor beckoned to them. The detectives followed him back into the room.

'My client agrees to give a DNA sample,' said Lucas. 'However, unless he is under arrest, we insist that he is not kept in custody while we wait for the result.'

'Fair enough,' said Harris. 'It is likely to take several days for the results to come back anyway. He'll be bailed under investigation. The sergeant here will make the necessary arrangements.'

Gallagher led the solicitor and his client away and, with the task completed, headed for the inspector's office half an hour later.

'Just the person,' said Harris as Gallagher walked into the room. 'Doc has just been on. He wants us to see him at Roxham General. He's got a cause of death for us. He sounded quite pleased with himself.'

Chapter seven

It did not take Harris and Gallagher long to make the journey down the valley to the county town of Roxham in the inspector's Land Rover and they were soon standing in the mortuary at the General Hospital, where Professor Rokeby had laid the skeleton out on the examination table.

'What you got for us then?' asked Harris.

'I think we can say with a degree of confidence that we're looking at a murder,' said the pathologist.

'How do you know that?'

'Well, like I said, I called in a pal of mine and we worked on it until well past eleven last night.' He paused and looked at the detectives. 'No, don't thank me.'

'I'll get a medal struck,' said Harris.

'I don't know,' said the pathologist with a good-natured sigh. 'Nobody appreciates me these days.'

'I appreciate you,' said Gallagher. 'What do you do again?'

'Yes, thank you, Sergeant,' said Professor Rokeby. He leaned over the skeleton. 'We know it's murder because, if you look really closely, you can just make out a few hairline fractures on the neck. It was my pal that noticed them first.'

He moved aside to let the detectives see for themselves.

'His eyesight must be better than mine,' said Gallagher.

'Well, they're there, alright,' said the pathologist. He passed the sergeant a magnifying glass. 'Here, try this.'

Gallagher looked closer.

'So they are.' The sergeant passed the glass to Harris for the inspector to take a look of his own.

'Cause?' asked Harris.

'They're consistent with force being applied,' said Professor Rokeby. 'I'd say she was strangled. My pal reckons it could have happened any time between the seventies and the early nineties.'

'Good work, Doc,' said Harris. He gave the pathologist an approving nod. 'How long will it take to get the DNA results back so we can identify her?'

'The lab's backed up with work but I know the director and he's promised to do what he can to push things through a bit quicker, in return for a nice single malt. It could still be a few days, though. Like he says, he's got a room full of samples all marked "Urgent". And your "Urgent" is at least thirty years old.'

'So, what do we do in the meantime?' asked Gallagher. He looked at Harris. 'We haven't got anywhere near enough to arrest Haynes, have we?'

'I'm not sure it's anything to do with him, anyway,' said the inspector. 'If he was worried about the body being found, why draw attention to himself like he has? And if he wanted to move it before it was discovered, he had plenty of opportunity to do so without anyone knowing.'

Harris looked at the skeleton.

'The Press Office has suggested I make a direct appeal for information through the media,' he said. 'Someone must have missed her.'

'You'll like that,' said Gallagher. 'Your favourite people.'

* * *

44

Harris made his appeal early that afternoon, standing on the steps in front of the police station to address the journalists. He did not know what reaction the event would illicit but by the time he had concluded his final interview, the first phone call had been received in the CID squad room. By the time the inspector arrived, the team had received seven calls. An eighth came in as Harris entered the room and saw that every available officer was on the phone. The inspector watched in disbelief for a few moments then headed for Alistair Marshall, who had just replaced his receiver.

'Surely these aren't all to do with the press conference, are they?' asked Harris.

'They are, yes,' said the detective constable. 'That call was from a woman who saw your press conference live on Sky News. She lives in Birmingham and her daughter went missing twenty-nine years ago. Disappeared on the way home from a pub one night. The boyfriend was questioned but released for lack of evidence.'

'What's the link with our area?' asked Harris.

'None that I can see.'

'So, why's she ringing up then?'

'Hope,' said Gillian Roberts, who had entered the room and caught the back end of the conversation. 'Or desperation. Take your pick. As far I can see, none of the disappearances have any links with our area. Quite a few of the women were not even blonde.'

'So why contact us then?' asked Harris.

'If you had children, you'd understand. I suspect that the parents spend their lives waiting for the next body to turn up.' The mother of two teenage boys herself, Roberts shook her head sadly. 'Imagine living your life not knowing where your child is. It doesn't bear thinking about, it really doesn't.'

Another phone rang.

'I'll get it,' said Sally Orr, who had just finished her call. She pressed a button on her phone. 'Levton Bridge CID, Detective Constable Orr.'

The young detective started to write on her notepad.

'And your daughter's name is?' she asked. 'And she went missing where? The Isle of Wight. When was this?'

Harris shook his head again and noticed that Butterfield had finished her call.

'Anything?' he asked.

'Don't think so,' said Butterfield. She glanced down at her notepad. 'Seventeen-year-old went missing after a party in South London thirty-three years ago.'

'We'll have to check them all out,' said Roberts. 'God knows how we're going to do it, mind. They were all on index cards.'

'We could end up wasting a lot of time,' said Harris.

'We could indeed,' said Roberts. 'But our Jane Doe could be in there somewhere. And we have to check them out even if we know that they're nothing to with Meadowview House. After all, we *did* ask the families to get in touch.'

Another desk phone rang.

'Hope,' said Roberts as she watched another officer pick up the receiver, 'it's a terrible thing.'

Harris's mobile rang and he took the call.

'Ross,' he said. 'I'm a bit busy, can I ring you back?'

'You might want to listen to what I have to say now,' said the Wildlife Trust director. 'I think I may have some information on the young woman at Meadowview House.'

Harris looked round the room; every officer was again engaged in conversation.

'You and the whole world,' he said.

'Yes, but I suspect that no one else has got a picture of her.'

'On my way,' said Harris.

Chapter eight

Harris and Gallagher headed back down the valley to a woodland nature reserve on the outskirts of Roxham, where the inspector parked the Land Rover outside a single-storey timber-framed building with solar panels on its roof. Having walked into the headquarters of the Three Valleys Wildlife Trust, the detectives announced themselves at reception and were taken to see Ross Makin. Also in the director's office was a young, dark-haired bespectacled woman, who was wearing a pleated skirt and a brown cardigan.

'Can I introduce you to Hannah Crosby?' said Makin once the officers were seated. 'She's the one who turned up the picture. Show them, Hannah.'

Crosby opened a brown file lying on the desk in front of her and produced a colour photograph which showed a young woman with short blonde hair and freckles. She was wearing jeans and a floral T-shirt and leaning against a fence, which Harris recognised immediately as the one running behind Meadowview House.

Crosby slid the picture across the desk to the detectives and as they studied the woman's smiling features, the officers were struck by how happy she looked. Both men experienced a strong sensation that they were looking at the woman whose skeleton had been discovered under the floorboards at the house, that they were viewing a snapshot depicting a time of innocence before the wicked act that so cruelly snuffed out her life.

'Where was it found?' asked Harris.

'It fell out of one of the natural history books which George Stillwell owned,' said Makin. 'You will have seen them when you went to the house as a teenager. On the shelves in the living room.'

Harris nodded.

'Well, they've been sitting in boxes in our back office for months,' said Makin. 'Some of them are very old and very rare and just about every one of them is long since out of print. It's quite an important collection. Remarkable when you think that everyone viewed George as a simple north-countryman. Hannah is a freelance archivist and, once I knew that we had the funding, I hired her to catalogue the books. We're going to create a library in the new visitor centre. We were going to name it in George's honour but I'm not so sure now.'

'It may still be alright,' said Harris.

'I hope so. Don't tell anyone about the idea, though, it's going to be our big surprise announcement when we open the centre.'

'Your secret is safe with me,' said Harris. He gave Makin a rueful look. 'Talking of secrets, I guess now is the time when I admit that I took several of the books when we used to hang out there?'

Gallagher raised an eyebrow at his boss.

'Graffiti, criminal damage and now the theft of rare books?' he said with a slight smile. 'You were a right one-man crimewave, weren't you?'

'I just didn't want to see them ruined,' said Harris. 'Besides, I only took three or four of them. I've still got them if you want them back, Ross?'

'No, you keep them,' said Makin. 'You can regard them as a token of our appreciation for the support you have given us. In fact, it's just as well you did take them. We had to throw out quite a few after thirty years of sitting in a damp house. We salvaged most of them, though.'

Harris looked at the picture of the young woman again.

'Anything to indicate who she is?' he asked.

'There's no name or address but this may help,' said Crosby. She turned the picture over to reveal a handwritten message.

'My dearest George,' she read out loud. 'Thank you for seeing us when we came to the house, particularly since we disturbed you by arriving unannounced. I thought you would like to see the picture taken on the day. It was fascinating to see the meadows and you deserve all credit for preserving them. The experience has proved extremely helpful background for the dissertation on upland flora that I hope to write in my final year. I may return sometime to do more research. I do hope that will be acceptable. Love, R.'

'I think we can safely assume that she did come back,' said Gallagher grimly. 'But that this time she didn't leave.'

'So it would seem,' said Harris. 'Do any of our missing women have names beginning with R?'

'Not that I recall. Clearly, she was a student, though.'

'We'll need to identify all the places that were running botany courses at the time,' said Harris.

'Ah, well, I may be able to help there,' said Makin. 'When I was looking for somewhere to do my natural sciences degree, I checked out universities and quite a few of them offered botany modules. I can jot you down a list, if it would help.

'It would,' said Harris. 'Thank you.'

'Then there was the Henderson Institute of Botany, of course,' said Hannah Crosby. 'Don't forget that.'

'Where was that based?' asked Gallagher.

'It was set up in London by the nineteenth-century botanist Gerald Henderson,' said Crosby. 'It closed in 1998, a couple of years after celebrating its centenary. The archive went to the University of South East London.'

'How come you know so much about it?' asked the sergeant.

'From when I was doing my master's. It was one of the case studies for the assessment on what happens to historical records when places close. The University of South East London took more than a thousand books and documents.'

'We should definitely include it on the list,' said Harris. He looked at Gallagher, who nodded. 'Hopefully, one of them can give us a lead on who she was.'

'And who accompanied her to Meadowview House,' said Gallagher.

'Find the answer to that and we may well find our killer,' said Harris.

'So, you're sure it's a murder then?' said Makin gloomily.

'I am afraid so,' said Harris. 'It'll be a while before your people can get back in to resume the work.'

'Let's hope someone recognises the woman in the photograph then,' said Makin.

Chapter nine

By the time Jack Harris arrived at Levton Bridge Police Station for work the next morning, the number of phone calls to the CID squad room from hopeful parents had reached nineteen. Having arranged to do a catch-up with Gillian Roberts once he had checked his emails, the inspector walked into his office, gave the dogs some treats from his top drawer and settled down behind his desk.

He had just switched on his computer when his mobile phone rang. The inspector frowned at the distraction but smiled when he saw the caller's name: in addition to being head of the Economic Crime Unit at Greater Manchester Police, Detective Inspector Jenny Armannsson had been his girlfriend for two years after they met during an investigation involving their respective forces. It was the first settled relationship he had experienced and had surprised those who knew his reputation as something of a ladies' man.

'Now then,' said Harris, taking the call. He tipped back on his chair and put his feet up on the desk. 'What can I do for you?'

'The television news said that you are treating your skeleton as a murder and I thought that you could do with a bit of help. Do I take it that you are still interested in this Haynes fellow?'

'We certainly are. Have you got something on him? I could do with an excuse to bring him back in on a more formal basis.'

'Well, this may help. One of my team saw a report last night on Sky News which mentioned his claim to own Meadowview House and recognised the MO. There was a similar case down here a few years back, a complaint from a children's charity that had been bequeathed a Victorian villa in Oldham by an elderly woman who died without living relatives. After the charity went public with its plans to turn the house into a children's centre, the chief executive received a visit from a man calling himself Michael Staples, who claimed that the old dear was his grandmother and that the house was really his. Sound familiar?'

'Does it ever?' Harris lowered the chair legs to the ground and sat forward. 'What happened?'

'Staples kept pestering the chief executive for weeks – even ignored the threat of an injunction against him – so the charity reported the incident to us.'

'And what did your people do?' asked Harris.

'Pretty much what you've done. Staples could not produce any evidence to back up his claim but we couldn't disprove what he was saying either, so we warned him off instead. He must have realised that he wasn't getting anywhere because the charity never heard from him again.'

'Are you sure it's the same man?'

'The Sky report featured a picture of Haynes so we ran a screenshot past the chief executive and he said that it looked like him.'

'That's very interesting,' said Harris.

'That's not the half of it,' said Armannsson. 'Another member of our team remembered another case eleven years ago. A detached house in Salford, which was going to be turned into an art gallery by a charitable trust. They were approached by a man using the same MO. That one was marked NFA but I've emailed the details in case you want to see the two chief executives together. If you do, I'd quite like to be involved.'

'No problem. Maybe we can see them today?'

'I'm certainly available. While I've got you, I take it you don't want me to come and see you this weekend, given everything that's been happening?'

'I'm not sure how much I'll be round,' said the inspector. 'I think we'll have to cancel.'

'Pity, I was looking forward to a romantic weekend stuck halfway up a hill in a draughty cottage which last saw a duster the last time I was there,' said Armannsson.

Harris was still chuckling at the joke when Gillian Roberts walked into the room, clutching a sheaf of papers.

'And what's amused you then?' said the detective inspector. She sat down and scratched Scoot and Archie on the head as the dogs came to welcome her, their tails wagging furiously.

'Just something Jenny said,' replied Harris. 'She's emailing me details of other cases involving Haynes. It looks like he's a serial scammer.'

'We could certainly do with some kind of a breakthrough.' Roberts gestured to the pile of papers, which she had now placed on the desk. 'I'm not sure there's anything of use in these missing women reports.'

'None of them involving a woman whose name begins with R then?'

'I am afraid not. We've had calls ranging from Devon to Aberdeen but none of the women had any links with this area either. And no one has mentioned an interest in botany. We sent the families scans of the photograph but no one recognised her. I guess we could release the picture to the news outlets?'

'I'd like to find out more about her ourselves before we do that,' said Harris. 'I don't like running investigations through the media. Makes them feel like they're setting the agenda.'

'Well, we have to be seen to be doing something. We'll only add to the families' anguish if we handle it wrong, particularly if they tell a journalist. There's already a lot of speculation on social media.'

'Can't the forces who handled the original missing persons reports help us out?'

'Most of them take the view that we made our bed so we can lie in it,' said Roberts. 'Besides, by and large, they can't lay their hands on the records. We're the first police force to take an interest in years. I fear that you're going to have to ask headquarters for more officers, if this carries on.'

'I'd rather not. The top floor are already worried that the case will overwhelm us and I can't risk whoever has been stirring things up against me telling the chief that I've lost control of the investigation. My money's on Alan Jay.'

'He's always been a sneaky little so-and-so,' said Roberts. 'And he detests you.'

Harris looked up hopefully as there was a knock on the open door and Sally Orr entered the office, clutching a notepad.

'Sorry to interrupt,' she said.

'That's OK,' said Harris. He gestured for her to take a seat. 'What you got?'

'The sarge suggested that I update you on educational centres that ran courses that included botany. I've tracked down fifteen of them so far. Trouble is, just about all the records from that time were paper-based and have long since been lost.'

'Anything on this Henderson Institute?'

The young constable glanced down at her notepad.

'It closed in 1998, citing falling student numbers,' said the constable. 'Most of its students transferred to the University of South East London, which was just round the corner. I've been talking to a young woman in admin.'

'Does she know if the staff transferred over as well?' asked Roberts. 'If we can't track down any of the students, maybe we can find out if any of the lecturers accompanied our Jane Doe to Meadowview House?'

'The woman at the university hasn't got any names apart from the director, a chap called' – Orr ran a finger down the page – 'Professor Gordon Nesbitt. He'll be elderly now, assuming he's still alive.'

'Gordon Nesbitt,' mused Harris. 'Now that rings a bell.'

'Why?' asked Roberts.

'Not sure but I've definitely heard the name before. It'll come to me, probably when I'm out walking the dogs. That's when it usually happens.'

Chapter ten

Harris and Gallagher recognised the bewilderment that they had previously witnessed on Ross Makin's face as they sat in the office of the director of the children's charity in Oldham. It was 3:00pm that afternoon and they were at the Victorian villa that had eventually been converted into a children's centre, despite the best efforts of Geoffrey Haynes to derail the proposal. The happy cries of youngsters playing outside was in sharp contrast to the mood exhibited by David Ledbitter, an earnest bespectacled young man who viewed them with an anxious look on his face. Sitting next to him was Amanda Scarff, the chief executive of the art gallery in Salford, and also present was a woman who had short blonde hair and was wearing a dark business suit. It was Jenny Armannsson, who spoke first.

'We are sorry to have brought back such painful memories,' she said. 'We know you would rather forget Geoffrey Haynes.'

'I certainly had rather hoped that all this was behind us,' said Ledbitter. 'However, I was not really surprised to receive the call. I guessed it would be about the skeleton under the floorboards.'

'What makes you say that?' asked Harris.

'I recognised Haynes when he gave an interview on the television news. And I recognised the story that he used to try to trick the Wildlife Trust. I was considering whether or not to ring you, anyway.'

'So, why didn't you?' asked Harris.

'I don't want the charity's name dragged into something like that,' said Ledbitter. 'Funders can be very sensitive when it comes to bad publicity. I'm sure you understand.'

Harris recalled the expressions on people's faces when Haynes interrupted Ross Makin's speech at Meadowview House. He understood, alright, and frowned – he had little time for such views, preferring to confront the truth wherever he found it. However, before he could reply, there was a particularly loud shout from outside and the moment passed and delight momentarily banished the troubled expression from Ledbitter's face.

'Such a lovely sound,' he said with a smile. 'If ever I get down about things, I think of the children we are helping. Do any of you have kids?'

Armannsson shot Harris the slightest of looks. Children were not in his plans and Jenny had assured him that she felt the same way, but they had uncomfortably skirted around the subject on several occasions as their relationship deepened. Gallagher noticed the look between them and gave a slight smile; whenever anyone mentioned the idea of his boss becoming a father, he would reply that the prospect of another Jack Harris in the world was not one that he wished to contemplate.

Acutely conscious that the charity officials were looking expectantly at the detectives and expecting one of them to speak, the sergeant broke the silence as more squeals of laughter filtered through to the office.

'What's the story with the children who use this place?' he asked.

'An all too familiar one, I am afraid,' said Ledbitter. 'Missing fathers, mothers incapable of caring for them, that sort of thing. This place is one of the few constants in their lives. That's why I was so angry when this fellow tried to take it away from us. Such a cruel thing to do.'

'He does seem to target charities,' said Gallagher. 'Exactly what happened?'

'He turned up at our offices one morning and demanded to see me,' said Ledbitter. 'Wouldn't take no for an answer and made such a scene that I let him in, which is when he claimed that this place belonged to him.'

'Same story with us,' said Scarff. 'He was very rude to the girl on reception. She was in tears.'

Gallagher reached into his jacket pocket and produced a screenshot of Haynes giving an interview to the television news. The sergeant slid it across the desk towards her.

'Is that him?' he asked.

Amanda Scarff nodded.

'Only he didn't call himself Geoffrey Haynes,' she said. 'He claimed that his name was Dennis Marriott. The old lady who left us her house was called Marjorie Marriott. We assume that he got the name from reports in the local media. He said that Marjorie was his great aunt.'

'He introduced himself as Michael Staples when he came to see us,' said Ledbitter, 'but he claimed that his real name was Bradley Johnson. The woman who bequeathed the house to us was Gladys Johnson and the media had named her as well. He said he'd spent his childhood in foster homes but that she was his grandmother.'

'I take it he did not show you any paperwork to prove his claim?' said Armannsson. 'A birth certificate, anything like that?'

'How could he?' said Scarff. 'There isn't anything. The will was uncontested and we took everything through the proper legal channels. Until he walked into my office, I'd never heard of Dennis Marriott.'

'And when you told him that, what did he say?' asked Harris.

'Have you met him?' asked Scarff.

Harris nodded.

'Then you know what the man's like and imagine how he reacted,' said Scarff. 'He made a real pest of himself for a few weeks. He was quite aggressive and, in the end, we called in the police. We didn't see him after that, thank goodness. Do you think he killed this poor young woman? I mean, I know he can get angry but he didn't look the type to kill anyone.'

'Crippen looked like an accountant,' said Gallagher.

Scarff gave him a sick look.

* * *

An hour later, with the interview concluded, the three detectives left Oldham and headed for a service station close to the M6, where they settled down at a corner table with their hot drinks.

'So,' said Armannsson. She took a sip of coffee and looked at Harris, who was topping up his mug from the teapot. 'What now?'

'God knows how he fits into our investigation,' said the inspector. 'But I'm more convinced than ever that we dismissed him too readily.'

Gallagher nodded.

'We should have arrested him when we had the chance,' said the sergeant. He reached for his scone. 'He's a con man through and through. However, one thing puzzles me. I mean, as con men go, he's not very good, is he? Like he himself said, any decent con man would forge some documents but he's done none of that. And of the three attempts we know about, none was successful. Why keep trying if it never works?'

'Maybe it has worked elsewhere and we just don't know about it,' said Armannsson.

'Maybe,' said Harris. 'Or maybe he's not a con man. Maybe he genuinely believes all the stuff that he spouts. Maybe we're looking at a fantasist and one with an aggressive streak. That could make him dangerous.'

His mobile phone rang. He took the call and listened for a few moments before placing the device on the table.

'That was Sally,' he said. 'The fostering people have no record of a Ken and Marion. We need our Haynes in for questioning PDQ.'

'Do you know where he is?' asked Armannsson.

'If you ask me, he's gone to ground,' said Gallagher. 'He'd have assumed that the interviews he gave to the media would only be carried locally but suddenly it's national news. He won't have bargained on that. I reckon he's spooked.'

Attempts to track down Haynes during the remainder of the day provided no encouragement. Gallagher rang his mobile number repeatedly on the journey back to Levton Bridge but the device remained switched off and when the sergeant phoned the solicitor in Carlisle, the lawyer said that he had not heard from his client since their meeting at Levton Bridge Police Station. A check with Gallagher's friend in the Metropolitan Police confirmed that Haynes had still not gone home.

'Geoffrey Haynes,' said Gallagher as he walked into the inspector's office just before 7:00pm, 'is well and truly in the wind.'

So, it was only later that evening that a frustrated Jack Harris turned his thoughts back to the Henderson Institute of Botany and the professor whose name he had recognised earlier in the day. The inspector tried to place him as he drove the several miles out of Levton Bridge along the main valley road towards his home. However, he had come up with nothing by the time he reached the winding track which took him to his cottage halfway up Dead Hill.

Harris had stumbled across the property not long after moving back to the area when he and Scoot – the inspector had just the one dog at the time – were out on a summer evening walk. He had bought the cottage for a knock-down price and spent the next few months carrying out renovations. He was attracted by the fact that, when he looked out of the living room window, all he could see were fields grazed by sheep and, stretching away above them, the summits of the hills, which were so often obscured by cloud. Something about the fact that he so rarely saw people – the shepherd, the odd hiker, that was about it – appealed to something deep within Jack Harris and he felt at home in the cottage.

Having parked the Land Rover, the inspector gave the dogs their tea then took them for a walk, guiding their way along the paths with a torch even though all three of them instinctively knew every step. Walk finished, they returned to the cottage where Harris lit the fire in the living room and made himself something to eat. With his meal consumed, he settled down in the armchair and sipped from his glass of whisky as he turned the events of the day over and over in his mind. And, as he did so, he came back time and time again to the name Professor Gordon Nesbitt.

'Nesbitt, Nesbitt,' he murmured. He placed his glass on the side table and walked over to the bookshelves that lined one of the walls. Just about every one of the books on display was about flora and fauna, it was all Jack Harris read, and he ran his finger along the spines. 'Come on, show yourself. You're in there somewhere, I know it.'

He was right. Although none of the titles bore the professor's name, something made the inspector halt at one of the books he had purloined from Meadowview House all those years before, a tatty volume with a torn cover which bore the faded image of a flower and the title *A Study of the Upland Meadows of the North Pennines.*

'I wonder,' he said, taking the book down from the shelf.

Harris turned to the contents page, noting that each chapter had been written by somebody different. Running his eye down the list of authors, he found what he was looking for and gave a smile of satisfaction. Filled with an increasing sense that he had found something of importance, the inspector flicked through the pages of the book until he reached the chapter called *A Case Study on the Benefits of Upland Meadow Conservation*, written by Professor Gordon Nesbitt. The first page was dominated by a black-and-white photograph which Harris realised showed the same spot on the hillside behind Meadowview House where the young woman in the photograph had had her picture taken. He read the opening lines of the article.

'One of the finest examples of surviving upland meadows in the North Pennines are to be found at Meadowview House,' he read. 'The house lies twenty miles to the east of the market town of Levton Bridge and is owned by one George Stillwell, a solitary individual and a north-countryman through and through, who has devoted his life to the preservation of the meadows that lie behind his cottage. A visit to the site is a delight, allowing the visitor to step back in time…'

Harris stopped reading.

'I wonder if any of his students had a name beginning with R,' he said thoughtfully.

He carried the book over to the armchair, sat down, reached for his glass and resumed his reading.

Chapter eleven

A purposeful Jack Harris was back at the police station early the next morning and by 8:00am he had called his team together. The detectives sat at the large table in the briefing room and watched expectantly as Harris held up the dog-eared book and told them what he had discovered.

'It could well lead us nowhere,' he concluded, 'but Meadowview House is not known to most people so anyone with links to the property has got to be worth pursuing. Sally, has your desk search turned anything up on Nesbitt yet?'

'He seems to have dropped out of sight after the Henderson Institute closed down,' said the constable.

'Keep trying,' said Harris. 'But remember that Nesbitt is only one of three lines of inquiry. Matty lad, any updates on Geoffrey Haynes?'

'Nothing overnight,' said Gallagher. 'Not even any ANPR hits on his car.'

'I assume the third line of inquiry is Old Man Stillwell?' said Butterfield.

'He's still got to be the main suspect,' said Harris. 'We know that he did not welcome visitors. Maybe when our Jane Doe went back, George lost his rag and killed her.'

Butterfield looked as if she was about to speak but thought better of it. The gesture was not lost on Harris.

'If you've got something to say, say it,' he said.

Butterfield glanced at Gallagher, mindful of his previous warnings about the way that she spoke to senior officers. The sergeant nodded; *phrase it carefully*, said his expression.

'Well?' said Harris.

'It's just that I'm not sure about George being a murderer,' said Butterfield. She tried to sound as respectful as possible. 'Nothing I hear about him suggests that he was violent. Grumpy, antisocial, reclusive, yes, possibly even paranoid, but not violent. Killing our Jane Doe would be out of character.'

Everyone waited to see how the inspector would react at being contradicted by a junior officer but he nodded in agreement.

'I suspect that you may well be right but for the moment, we keep him in the frame.' Harris clapped his hands and stood up. 'OK, folks, you know what you have to do.'

His mobile phone rang and he fished the device out of his jacket pocket and took the call.

'Doc,' he said. 'You're up and about bright and early. You got some news for us?'

'Certainly have.' Harris could sense the barely suppressed excitement in the pathologist's voice. 'We've had a DNA hit on your Jane Doe. Suffice to say that you have no idea who you've got on your hands.'

'She was a student,' said Harris.

'That's not the half of it,' said Professor Rokeby. 'But I'd rather not discuss it on the phone. Can you come and see me?'

* * *

Less than an hour later, an intrigued Harris and Gallagher were sitting in the pathologist's office at

Roxham General Hospital, nursing mugs of tea. The pathologist's eyes gleamed as he looked at them across his desk; he had the air of a man with big news to impart and he was enjoying himself.

'I thought you said it was highly unlikely we'd get a DNA match for our Jane Doe,' said Harris.

'What I said was that I didn't expect to find a direct match. However, if you recall, I also said that we might get lucky with someone else on the database and we did.'

'So why the big mystery?' asked Harris. 'Who is she?'

Professor Rokeby allowed himself a dramatic pause before replying; he was relishing the thought of the impact that his revelation would have on the inspector and was reluctant to let the moment pass too quickly.

'Let's just say that her father is someone from your past,' said the pathologist. 'You may not actually have met him, but I suspect you will have heard the name during your days investigating gangland crime.'

'Really?' said Harris. 'Who is it?'

'Davie Grogan.'

Harris stared at him in astonishment.

'Are you sure?' he said.

'Computer says yes.' The pathologist grinned. 'Her DNA shows a familial match with samples taken from both Davie and his sons when they were arrested in 2005.'

The pathologist beamed as the inspector appeared to be struggling to articulate a response.

'Good, eh?' he said.

'It's bloody amazing,' said Harris. He shook his head in disbelief. 'But what on earth is Davie Grogan's daughter doing hidden beneath the floorboards of Meadowview House?'

'That's for you to find out,' said Professor Rokeby. He reached for his mug. 'I've done my bit.'

'Would someone care to tell a humble sergeant exactly what is going on?' said Gallagher. 'Who is Davie Grogan when he's at home?'

'Davie Grogan,' said Harris, 'was one of the leading gangland figures in Glasgow in the eighties and nineties. He and his boys were into anything you care to name, drugs, firearms, protection rackets, robbery, the lot. And they were a vicious lot. Nobody crossed the Grogans unless they were looking to get themselves slashed.'

'They sound a right bunch of charmers,' said Gallagher.

'They were indeed,' said Harris. 'There was a third boy, Robbie, who was killed in a knife fight in a city centre bar. Something about a drug deal gone wrong, as I recall.'

'And you heard about the Grogans when you worked in Manchester, did you?' said Gallagher.

'More than heard about them, Matty lad. Doc's right that I never met Davie but I did cross swords with the boys.'

'Really?' said the pathologist. 'How come?'

'We heard that Davie's boys planned to meet some of our local ne'er-do-wells in a Manchester city centre pub to discuss the supply of drugs. The Gangs Unit had not long been established and it seemed like an excellent way to put down a marker.'

'Why were they looking to Manchester?' asked Gallagher.

'Because they lost their place in the hierarchy in Glasgow when they were in prison,' said Harris. 'Davie's health was not that good when he came out of Barlinnie, so he took more of a back seat and Angus stepped up. He could see that there were too many young tyros competing to be top dog so he decided that it made sense to expand away from Glasgow. Angus has always been the strategist – Rory's more of a hot-head – and because he had contacts in Manchester, it was the obvious choice.'

'And what happened?' asked Gallagher.

'We went in mob-handed. Kicked in a few doors, broke a few noses and blacked a few eyes. The Grogans had a night in the cells for their trouble then hightailed it back north with their tails between their legs but they'd got the message and it all fizzled out and they didn't come back. The boys were livid – it was a massive loss of face for them.'

'Two more off your Christmas card list,' said Gallagher.

'Indeed,' said Harris. He looked at Professor Rokeby. 'Davie must be an old fellow now? Assuming he's still alive.'

Rokeby glanced down at his piece of paper.

'If he is, he'll be eighty-three.' The pathologist ran his finger down the sheet of paper. 'The boys are no spring chickens either. Angus is coming up to sixty and Rory's not far behind him.'

'But, surely, there can't be any connection between the Grogans and Old Man Stillwell?' said Gallagher

'You wouldn't have thought so,' replied Harris. 'I take it the records don't mention the daughter's name, Doc?'

'I am afraid not and I couldn't find anything about her going missing.'

'I've still got a couple of contacts up in Glasgow, so I'll put a call in,' said Harris. 'Thanks, Doc.'

'I'm not sure you should be thanking me,' said the pathologist. 'I fear that I have only made your life more complicated.'

'Everyone makes my life more complicated,' said Harris and headed for the door.

Chapter twelve

The next morning saw Harris and Gallagher sitting in a busy tearoom in the Sauchiehall Street area of Glasgow city centre just before 11:00am. Opposite them at the table was a man whose face was traced with lines that told the story of a police career well lived. The Levton Bridge officers had immediately been struck on meeting retired Detective Sergeant Malcom Gray by how nervous he appeared. He had insisted that they sit in the furthest corner from the street so that they were difficult to see through the window.

'The Grogan boys may not be the force they once were but they're still nasty bastards,' he explained, 'and you don't feel as safe once you're out of the job.'

Harris had heard similar views expressed during his days in Manchester and always took them seriously. 'We'll make this as quick as we can,' he told the former detective and received a nod of appreciation.

Gray glanced round to check that no one was listening before he started talking.

'So, you've found Rosie then,' he said. He kept his voice low to avoid being heard. 'That's a turn up for the books, after all these years. You sure it's her?'

Harris produced the photograph from his jacket pocket and placed it on the table. Gray examined the image for a few seconds before nodding.

'Looks like her,' he said. 'I never met her but I saw her on surveillance pictures taken at family gatherings. What's the story?'

Harris put the picture back into his pocket to prevent anyone passing the table from seeing it.

'We know that a woman whose name began with R visited the house and the skeleton's DNA matches the Grogans,' said Harris. 'There was a police record dating back to 2005.'

'The year we got them locked up,' said Gray. 'They got themselves involved in a fracas at a pub and a couple of their rivals ended up with serious injuries. Rory started it, by all accounts. Took exception to something that one of the men said. It was the only time we ever got them sent to prison. Angus was furious.'

'I'll bet he was,' said Harris. 'Trouble is, my team can't find anything about Rosie going missing. If the media covered the story, we've not been able to find any reports.'

'Nor will you.' Gray cut into his fruit scone and reached for the butter. 'The Grogans have never had anything to do with the police, they've always handled their own problems, so it was never reported officially.'

'But surely the police would have been able help track her down?' said Gallagher.

'Maybe we would but Davie did not want to give us an excuse to pry into his private life. He's always been paranoid.'

'So how old was Rosie when she went missing?' asked Gallagher.

'Just turned twenty-one,' said Gray. 'She vanished during the summer of 1993.'

'Which could make it a year or so after George Stillwell died,' said Gallagher, looking at Harris. 'And possibly after you and your mates stopped going to the house?'

'Sounds right,' said the inspector. 'Anyone we can talk to who can give us more information, Malcolm?'

'There's one or two folks,' said Gray. He took another nervous look round the tearoom then glanced at Harris. 'But you're not the most popular person with the Grogans and I hate to think what they will do if they hear that you are asking questions. They haven't forgotten the dust-up in Manchester. The Grogans are all about reputation and they lost face, thanks to you. I'll be honest, I thought twice about agreeing to meet you. I don't need hassle at my time of life.'

'I'll add Glasgow to the list of cities where people would rather I not visit then,' said Harris. 'They don't like me in Manchester, either.'

Although the inspector was smiling when he said it, and always contended that his unpopularity had never worried him, he did not take the risks lightly. He was careful whenever he returned to Manchester, either on police business or to see Jenny. The couple never dined out in the city, preferring pubs in villages that they knew they could trust. Harris poured himself a top-up of tea.

'So, what do we know about Rosie?' he asked.

'A nice kid, very studious. Always had her head in a book. Nothing like her brothers. Or her father. From what I've been told, she had a difficult relationship with Davie. She wanted nothing to do with the life that he envisaged for her, namely joining her mother in the kitchen. She wanted a career instead.'

'We think she was studying botany,' said Gallagher.

'She was, yes. She was fascinated by flowers as a child – she'd been inspired by seeing David Bellamy on the television and, by all accounts, she was always visiting Glasgow Botanic Gardens on Great Western Road, which might explain why she was at your house. According to the news reports I read, it's known for its meadows.'

'It is, yes,' said Harris. 'How did Davie react when she defied his wishes?'

'Badly.' Gray took a bite of scone and chewed for a couple of moments. 'He hated that people were saying that he could not even control his daughter. But she was a headstrong girl, was Rosie, and in the end, she got herself a grant and enrolled herself on a degree course in London.'

Gray produced a scrap of paper from his trouser pocket and passed it to Harris.

'A place called the Henderson Institute of Botany,' he said.

The Levton Bridge detectives exchanged glances; Gordon Nesbitt was, clearly, still in the frame.

'London's a long way from Glasgow,' said Gallagher. 'Did she not fancy anywhere closer to home?'

'The further away from Davie and the boys the better, I believe,' said Gray. 'She wanted to lead as independent a life as possible and there was always trouble whenever she came home.'

'How come no one at the university reported her missing?' asked Harris. 'Surely, alarm bells would have started ringing when she did not turn up for the new semester?'

'Students drop out all the time, don't they?' said Gray. 'Change course, switch universities, go to work at McDonald's instead.'

'These tensions between the family and Rosie,' asked Gallagher, 'were they serious enough for the Grogans to kill her?'

'They were capable of just about anything in those days but I'm not sure even the Grogans would go as far as killing their own flesh and blood,' said Gray. 'Besides, there were rumours about what happened to her.'

'Saying what?' asked Gallagher.

'What you've got to realise is that it was a febrile time in the city. Gangs fighting turf wars, tit-for-tat killings. There were plenty as thought that young Rosie was collateral damage. Kidnapped by a rival who then realised he had gone too far so killed her. Angus certainly thought

71

that's what happened, although no one ever admitted it. You wouldn't – you'd get Rory's blade between your shoulder blades for your trouble. For what it's worth, there's supposed to be an intelligence report from the time she disappeared, which lays all this out.'

'Can we see it?' asked Harris.

'God knows where it is. It was all hard copy in those days and a lot of stuff is missing. I'll ask for you.'

'Cheers,' said Harris. 'What do the Grogans do now, Malcolm? None of them are getting any younger.'

'The old man's well out of it. He lives in Dumfries and Galloway. Moved there with his wife a few years back. She died last year and he's in really poor health as well, apparently. Heart problems which started when he was in Barlinnie. From what we hear he's not that long for this world.'

'Oh, dear, what a pity, never mind,' said Harris. 'And the boys?'

'Desperately trying to persuade the city's underworld that they are still a force to be reckoned with, but no one's buying it and all they have is a few hangers-on. It's a young man's game, really.'

'You got an address for the old man?' asked Harris. 'We'll need to see him to break the news about his daughter.'

'I'd like to be a fly on that wall,' said Gray. 'I'll text you some directions. It can be a bit tricky to find.'

He looked towards the window and frowned as he noticed a man with slicked-back hair which was greying at the temples. He had been walking past the tearoom but had done a double-take when he spotted the detectives and was now standing outside, casting furtive looks in their direction.

'It appears that we've been spotted,' said Gray in a low voice. 'See that guy standing by the bin? The one trying to look natural?'

The Levton Bridge detectives followed his gaze and, just for a fleeting moment, Gallagher thought a look of recognition exchanged between the man and Harris. However, the inspector said nothing and Gallagher decided that he must have imagined it. Gray's anxiety, he concluded, must have communicated itself to him; Gallagher was never at ease when he and Harris found themselves in the world of organised crime. The inspector had too much of a record for winding villains up for the sergeant to be relaxed.

'Who is he?' asked Gallagher, continuing to look at the man.

'One of the Grogan's associates,' said Gray. 'John Foster. He's been on the scene since the early nineties but mainly on the periphery of things. However, just as I was retiring, our organised crime guys found out that Angus had started investing in his car showroom. They suspected that Foster was laundering money for the Grogans. It's only rumour, mind. Nothing has ever been proved. The force tried to bring a Proceeds of Crime action against him last year but it came to nothing.'

Gray noticed that Foster was talking into his mobile phone, drained his cup and stood up.

'Without wishing to sound rude,' he said. 'Might I suggest that it's time for you to fuck off out of our fair city? It wouldn't do to draw attention to yourselves any more than is necessary and English cops are even less popular than local ones, particularly when one of them is called Harris. I'm happily retired and have no desire to be involved with the Grogans, thank you very much.'

'I guess it might interfere with the golf swing,' said Harris.

Gray gave a slight smile.

'Something like that,' he said. 'Come on, let's go.'

Harris and Gallagher emptied their cups and the three men headed for the door, the inspector settling the bill on his way out. Having watched them emerge onto the street,

John Foster walked quickly away, preferring to observe from a distance as Harris and Gallagher shook Malcom Gray's hand and headed for the car park. The two Levton Bridge officers travelled in silence as Harris navigated the Land Rover through the busy city centre traffic and Gallagher only voiced his suspicion when the vehicle left Glasgow's outskirts on the southbound motorway.

'I had the impression that you recognised John Foster back there,' he said. 'And that he recognised you. Am I right?'

'I knew he ran a car showroom in the city but didn't know he was involved with the Grogans. It must be coming up thirty years since we last saw each other.'

'Thirty years?' Gallagher felt a knot tighten in his stomach. 'You must have been teenagers when you knew him then?'

'We were.'

'Why don't I really want to know any more?' said the sergeant.

'You know you said that things could get complicated? Well, they just did. Big time.' The inspector was silent for a few moments as he concentrated on guiding the Land Rover into the outside lane to pass a line of slow-moving vehicles. He only spoke when he had completed the manoeuvre. 'You see, John was one of the lads that played at Meadowview House when we were teenagers. It was his father's airgun we used to shoot at the outhouses.'

Gallagher closed his eyes for a second then opened them as a thought struck him.

'What about the other lads who you knocked about with?' he said. 'Any more of them gravitated to organised crime in Glasgow?'

'Not that I know of. Besides, there was only one of them went to the house with me and John. Barry's OK, though. I still get Christmas cards from him. Last I heard he was running a bar in Bournemouth.'

'Probably selling pina coladas to retired villains, knowing your friends,' said Gallagher sardonically. 'I take it you realise that you'll have to tell Curtis about Foster? Wait till Alan Jay hears about this.'

Harris did not reply and the sergeant's attempts to start another conversation came to nothing, so they travelled south in silence.

* * *

Once they were back at Levton Bridge Police Station, Harris called in at the divisional commander's office. Curtis looked up from the report he was reading when Harris entered the room.

'I'm afraid there's something you need to know,' said the inspector.

'Why do those words fill me with foreboding?' replied the commander.

'At least I'm telling you this time,' said Harris. 'You won't hear it from the janitor.'

Curtis gave a slight smile and gestured for the inspector to take a seat. Half an hour later, following an uncomfortable conversation with the commander, Harris had just walked into his office when the desk phone rang.

'More bad news, I imagine,' he murmured gloomily as he picked up the receiver. 'Hello, DCI Harris.'

'Jack, it's Ross Makin. I think I've managed to track down Professor Nesbitt. The Trust has a botany group – all grey-haired women in wide-brimmed hats – and one of them remembered him from when he came up here to research upland meadows thirty years ago. He visited several locations, including Meadowview House. I asked if any of the group know anything about a young woman but none of them do. However, get this, one of the women described Nesbitt as a bit creepy.'

'Creepy?' said Harris. 'How?'

'She thought that he was probably a bit of a lech. Eyeing up the women. Wandering hands. That sort of thing.'

'Will she talk to us?'

'She will,' said Makin. 'She's called Betty Lord. She's in her eighties now but bright as a button. I've emailed her details to you and the address she has for Nesbitt.'

'How come she has his address?' asked Harris.

'He sends her a Christmas card each year and the most recent one said he had moved into a residential home in North London.'

'Good work,' said Harris. 'Do you fancy a job as a detective?'

'I think not,' replied Makin. 'Far too stressful. Give me flowers any day.'

Chapter thirteen

Jack Harris had much to occupy his thoughts as he left his office shortly before 9:00am the next morning and headed towards the briefing room, with the dogs trotting, as ever, at his heels. Although it was only a short walk along the corridor, it provided the inspector with yet another thing to think about as he glanced out of the window and down into the back yard where he saw a wiry, bespectacled uniformed officer getting out of his car.

'Now there's a surprise,' he murmured.

Harris scowled as Chief Inspector Alan Jay made his way across towards the rear entrance to the building. Sensing that he was being watched, Jay glanced up and, for a second, their eyes locked before Jay gave a slight smile and continued on his way. It was, thought Harris, the self-satisfied smile of a man who knew something that he didn't. The inspector sighed and continued on to the briefing room, where his team had gathered. Gillian Roberts was just replacing one of the phone receivers as he entered.

'That was Doc,' she said. 'He's got the DNA result back on Geoffrey Haynes. As expected, no match with Rosie Grogan.'

'No surprise there,' said Harris. He took a seat and glanced at Gallagher. 'I assume that he's still missing?'

'I am afraid so,' said the sergeant.

'Well, let's keep looking,' said Harris. 'He needs questioning on the frauds but it's looking like we can rule him out for the murder. I reckon it comes down to a choice between a professor with wandering hands or a bunch of Glasgow ne'er-do-wells. Anyway, I'll make this quick before Curtis removes me from the inquiry.'

'Why should he do that?' said Gallagher. 'You told him that you're in the clear, didn't you?'

'I did, but I'm not sure that will be enough, Matty lad. Not now that John Foster's name has cropped up in our investigation. I've just seen Alan Jay parking his car. I am assuming that he's here to whisper more poison in the commander's ear. Anyway, until I am removed, let's try to proceed as normal. Matty lad, you and I will go to see Davie Grogan today. Tell him the sad news.'

Gallagher nodded and Harris turned his attention to Alison Butterfield and Sally Orr.

'I want you two to see Betty Lord and check out what she means by Professor Nesbitt being creepy,' he said. 'He's a definite person of interest and I want us to...'

His voice tailed off as the commander's secretary walked into the briefing room.

'I'm sorry to interrupt, sir,' she said, 'but Mr Curtis would like to see you.'

Harris sighed and headed for the door.

'Wish me luck,' he said.

Harris walked with heavy footsteps down to the office where Curtis and Alan Jay were waiting for him. Jay looked at Harris with what the inspector could only describe as an expression of triumph on his face. The expression faded with the inspector's first words as Harris looked at Curtis.

'We been using too much printer paper again?' he asked.

Jay glared at him.

'Now, now, Jack,' said Curtis. There was a slight twitch of his lips; the commander had enjoyed the joke. 'Close the door, will you?'

Harris did as he was requested and sat down.

'Alan has just come to tell us his good news,' said the commander.

'Good news?' said Harris suspiciously.

'Yes. Maeve Riley has decided to leave early so he has been promoted to acting superintendent and is taking over as interim head of the Professional Standards Unit until a permanent appointment can be made. Do you want to congratulate him?'

Harris said nothing but had the distinct impression that the commander was enjoying the encounter.

'Yes,' said Jay, giving Harris a hard look, 'and now that I am your senior officer—'

'Acting senior officer,' said Harris.

'As your senior officer,' repeated Jay, 'and head of the Professional Standards Unit—'

'Interim head,' said Harris.

Jay could not conceal his irritation.

'That kind of attitude is exactly what compromises your work for this force,' he said. 'And it will not help the situation.'

'What situation's that?' asked Harris. He tried to come over as genuinely confused.

'Don't play me for a fool,' said Jay. 'I have told your commander that, all things considered, it would be unwise for you to carry on leading the investigation into events at Meadowview House.'

'And why's that?' asked Harris.

'Isn't it obvious, man? You have a personal connection with the case. What if your friend is somehow tied up with the death of the young woman? Let's face it, Jack, you're hardly impartial on this one.'

'Nothing points to John being involved at this stage,' said Harris. 'And even if it did, no one has ever had reason to doubt my impartiality in the past.'

'Nevertheless, we must be seen to be doing the right thing,' said Jay. His voice had assumed a preaching tone. 'The days when we could take our responsibility to the public for granted are behind us. We must not only do the right thing but be seen to do the right thing and to be beyond reproach in order to properly preserve our partnership with the public. Isn't that right, Superintendent?'

'He's got a point, Jack,' said Curtis.

Harris looked bleakly at him and noted that the triumphant expression had returned to Jay's face. This time it was the commander's turn to wipe it off.

'However, I am not going to act on his recommendation,' said Curtis.

Jay stared at him in astonishment.

'You're not?' he said.

'I'm not, no.'

'But I thought you agreed with me?' said Jay.

'You hardly gave me a chance to say what I thought, Alan. You've hardly drawn breath since you sat down.'

Noticing Harris's surprised look, the commander gave him the slightest of winks then returned his attention back to Jay.

'And before you do your usual trick of getting on your high horse and riding off to complain to the chief,' said Curtis, 'you should know that he agrees with me.'

'He does?' said Jay in a hollow voice.

'He does.' Curtis noted that Jay had opened his mouth to protest. 'And I'd think very carefully about your next words. I'm sure you appreciate how it might look if, just minutes into your first morning on the job, you pick a fight with the chief constable, the commander of the largest division and the force's most successful detective.'

Jay closed his mouth, stood up and, without speaking, headed for the door. He turned to look back at Harris.

'You cut too many corners,' he said. 'And it'll catch up with you one day.'

Once he had gone, Harris gave the commander an appreciative look.

'Thank you, sir,' he said.

'Yes, well, I'm not having a little lickspittle like Alan Jay telling me how to do my job. But he's right, Jack, you do cut too many corners. Don't let me down.'

A couple of minutes later, Harris walked into the CID squad room.

'Come on, you lot,' he said. 'Stop lounging about! We've got work to do.'

The sound of the applause reverberated round the station and out into the yard where a shell-shocked Alan Jay heard it as he unlocked his car.

Chapter fourteen

Having left the dogs in the care of one of the office staff at Levton Bridge Police Station, Harris and Gallagher headed north, the inspector guiding the Land Rover onto the M6 then, just after they had crossed the Scottish border, taking the slip road onto the westbound A75 to Dumfries.

'Do they really need this many roundabouts?' Gallagher said as they entered the seventh and final one on the bypass round the town before finding themselves on the far side of Dumfries.

Harris gestured to his mobile phone, which was sitting in its cradle on the dashboard.

'Malcolm's directions for the house are in texts,' he said.

Gallagher flicked through the messages.

'Five miles on the right,' he said. 'Looks like the house is halfway up the hillside. Are we sure that he'll be in?'

'He'll be in,' said Harris. 'The man's dying.'

'I'll be honest,' said Gallagher, 'I know you like bumping heads with these characters, but part of me is hoping that he's not in. Seriously ill or not, Davie Grogan sounds a right psycho and if his boys are there as well...'

The sergeant did not finish the sentence and Harris said nothing. Gallagher was silent for a couple of minutes before speaking again as the landscape opened out to reveal a range of hills stretching away to their right.

'What's more,' he said, 'we're out of our jurisdiction, aren't we? It feels very exposed. Not much in the way of back-up if things kick off.'

'You underestimate me, Matty lad,' said Harris. He gave a slight smile as he glanced in his wing mirror. 'I've taken out a bit of insurance.'

'Insurance?'

'Take a look behind us,' said Harris.

Gallagher did as instructed and saw a black Audi flash its headlights three times. Harris flicked his hazards in return.

'Who's that?' asked Gallagher.

'An old pal of mine,' said Harris. 'The Grogans are not the only ones who can play hardball.'

The comment did little to ease the sergeant's concerns as the vehicles approached a sign which read "The Laurels". After they had turned off the A75 and made their way up a long and winding track, they eventually arrived at a set of ornate gates where the track gave way to a gravel drive, which led to a large white house standing in its own grounds. As the vehicles approached, the Audi dropped back and Harris brought the Land Rover to a halt next to a couple of new BMWs parked in front of the property.

'Who says crime doesn't pay?' said Gallagher.

'No one,' replied Harris.

'Fair enough,' said the sergeant as they got out of the Land Rover. He glanced at the BMWs, trying but failing to conceal the nervousness that he was experiencing. 'Do you think the cars belong to the boys?'

'I suspect so.' Harris shot him a sharp look. 'Relax, will you? It'll be OK. Just leave the talking to me.'

'Past experience suggests that's not really a reassuring thought,' said Gallagher. 'You've landed me in enough tight spots to last a lifetime.'

'And haven't I always got you out OK?'

'There's a first time for everything,' said Gallagher.

As the officers walked past the BMWs, they noticed that the cars had stickers in the rear window bearing the words "John Foster Motors, Glasgow". Arriving at the house, the inspector rang the bell and, after a few moments, the door was opened by a wiry ginger-haired man with darting eyes and sallow cheeks. His eyes widened when he saw Harris.

'What the...?' he began.

'Hello, Rory,' said Harris. 'Long time, no see.'

'What the fuck do you want?'

'To talk to your father.'

'Well, my father doesn't want to talk to you.'

Rory made as if to close the door but found it jammed by the inspector's foot.

'It's important,' said Harris.

Grogan looked at him suspiciously and still did not stand aside. Harris fished a copy of the photograph out of his jacket pocket and held it up.

'It's about Rosie,' he said.

Rory was about to reply when a lean man with thinning dark hair appeared at the end of the hallway.

'Who is it, Rory?' said Angus in a Glaswegian accent that was less pronounced than his brother's. He gave a thin smile as he saw Harris. 'Well, well, look who it is. We heard that you've been nosing around in Glasgow. What do you want?'

'To talk to your father about Rosie.'

'Dad's very ill,' said Angus. 'You can talk to me.'

'I'd rather talk to your father,' said Harris. 'He's next of kin.'

The brothers exchanged glances then Angus nodded at Rory, who stood aside to allow the detectives into the house. Once inside, they were ushered through to a spacious lounge where sat an elderly man, his body frail and hunched after years of illness. There was an oxygen bottle next to his armchair and he was breathing with the aid of a mask. Harris had never met Davie Grogan but recognised him from his photograph despite the sunken cheeks and hollow eyes that were evidence of his rapidly deteriorating condition. The inspector spent a couple of moments trying to equate Grogan's fearsome reputation with the shell of a man that now faced him while Gallagher's eyes never left his sons, who had taken up positions by the door, blocking the detectives' escape route.

'Who's this?' asked Davie. He peered at Harris over his oxygen mask. His voice was tremulous and punctuated by a rasping sound as he tried to catch his breath.

'Jack Harris,' said Angus. 'Says that he wants to talk to you.'

'Yes, well I don't want to talk to him,' said the old man. He wafted a hand towards the door. 'Get rid of him.'

'He says it's about Rosie.'

The old man looked suspiciously at Harris.

'What about her?' he asked.

'We think we've found her body,' said the inspector.

Davie Grogan considered the comment for a few moments then gestured, with a feeble waft of the hand, for the detectives to sit down on the sofa. As they did so, Harris perused Davie's face seeking emotion but found only suspicion.

'This had better not be your idea of a joke,' said the old man.

'I never joke about death,' said Harris.

'Where did you find her?' asked Angus.

'Under the floorboards of a derelict property twenty miles from Levton Bridge,' said Harris. 'It's called Meadowview House.'

'Never heard of it,' said the old man.

'There was something about it on the news earlier this week,' said Angus. 'But I very much doubt it's her. Why on earth would she be at a place like that?'

Harris held up the photograph of Rosie again.

'I assume we are right and that this *is* her?' he asked.

The brothers nodded and emotion finally flickered across the old man's face as tears glistened in his eyes.

'Where did you get that?' he asked after taking a few moments to gather his composure.

'We believe that it was taken when she visited the house,' said Harris.

'Yes, but that doesn't mean the skeleton is her,' said Angus. 'It could be anyone.'

'DNA says it's her,' said Harris. 'Or at least someone closely related to you. Who else could it be?'

The room fell silent apart from the old man's laboured breathing. The brothers watched him with looks of genuine concern.

'I always hoped she would be found before I died,' said Davie eventually. His voice was so low that the detectives had to lean forward to catch the words. 'That I could finally lay her to rest.'

The old man closed his eyes and slumped back in his chair. After a few moments, he opened his eyes again and looked at Harris.

'How did she die?' he asked.

'We believe she was strangled,' said Harris.

'Any idea who did it?' asked Angus.

'We've got one or two lines of inquiry,' said the inspector blandly. He decided not to mention the professor; he was wary of the Grogans' tendency to take the law into their own hands. 'Nothing definite, though.'

'Do you know why she was at the house?' asked Angus.

'Yes, and I am wondering if you do, too,' said Harris. Although not convinced that the Grogans were involved in the death, the detective's suspicious nature meant that he still wanted to gauge their reaction. 'I am thinking that perhaps you knew the skeleton was her the moment the news broke.'

'How dare you come into my home and suggest that we had something to do with Rosie's death!' exclaimed the old man. He had found new energy and his eyes flashed anger. 'You seem to be forgetting that I am the victim here. This is my daughter we are talking about.'

He looked at his sons.

'Get rid of these jokers,' he said.

'It'll be a pleasure,' said Rory. He took a step towards Harris. 'Fuck off out of here.'

'All in good time,' said the inspector.

'Now,' rasped Rory. 'Before I finish the job from Manchester.'

'As I recall, you ended up with a broken nose that day,' said Harris. The inspector stood up. 'You can hardly notice it now, mind.'

Rory hesitated; Jack Harris was a big man and he remembered the pain and humiliation caused when the inspector had slammed him into a wall during the raid on the Manchester pub. He also recalled the mocking laughter as members of rival gangs had poked fun at the brothers when they returned to Glasgow and stories circulated about the encounter. Rage took over and, moving rapidly, Rory produced a knife from his jacket pocket and took another step towards Harris. Gallagher felt his heart skip a beat. Harris stayed calm.

'I'd take a look out of the window before you do anything rash,' he said.

Rory hesitated and Angus walked over to the window, from which he saw three uniformed officers standing by the Audi. All three wore uniforms bearing the insignia of Police Scotland and two of them had handguns in holsters; Angus recognised one of the men from the raid in Manchester.

'So, let's just keep calm, shall we?' said Harris. He nodded at the knife. 'And put that away.'

Still, Rory hesitated. Angus turned back from the window and looked at his brother.

'Do as he says,' he said.

Rory reluctantly slipped the weapon back into his pocket and contented himself with glowering at the inspector.

'That's better,' said Harris. 'Now then, the sooner you answer my questions, the sooner we can be out of here.'

'We didn't kill Rosie,' said Angus. 'We loved her and we'd never do a thing like that. And we'd never heard about Meadowview House until it turned up on Sky News.'

'Then what did you think had happened to her?' asked Harris, 'We heard that there were rumours that a rival gang might have done it. Is that what you believed had happened?'

'Malcolm Gray tell you that, did he?' said Angus. 'And don't deny that you've been talking to him. You were seen with him in a coffee shop off Sauchiehall Street.'

'By John Foster, yes, I know.'

Angus looked surprised.

'You know him?' he asked, looking suspiciously at the inspector. 'He said he only recognised you off the television.'

Harris had to think quickly; he had uttered the words without thinking and they immediately felt like a mistake that could put his old friend at risk.

'We grew up together,' said Harris. He tried to sound casual, like it didn't matter. 'But I hadn't seen him for the best part of thirty years until yesterday.'

It was time to change the subject.

'So, what did you do about the rumours when Rosie went missing, Angus?' he asked.

Before Angus could reply, his father's body was wracked by a bout of coughing and he doubled up, spitting phlegm into his oxygen mask. The door opened and a nurse walked quickly into the room and went over to the old man. Once she had tended to him, she looked accusingly at Harris.

'I think you had better go,' she said. 'Mr Grogan doesn't need this. He's very ill and stress only makes him worse.'

'Fair enough,' said Harris. 'We'll see ourselves out.'

The inspector headed for the door, followed by a relieved Gallagher. For a second it looked as if Rory would block their way, but after a look from Harris, he moved aside.

'When can we have Rosie's remains back?' asked Angus as the detectives walked into the hallway. 'We need to arrange the funeral.'

'When I say so,' said Harris. A thought struck him and he looked back at the old man, who had closed his eyes as he attempted to breathe. 'I'm sorry for your loss, Davie.'

The old man did not reply; both of them knew that the inspector did not mean it.

As the detectives left the house, Harris turned back to Angus, who was standing on the doorstep.

'So, now that it's obvious that a rival gang didn't take Rosie, who do you think killed her?' asked Harris.

'Goodbye, Chief Inspector,' said Angus. He gestured at the waiting uniformed officers. 'And get them off my father's property.'

He slammed the front door closed and Harris gave a slight smile and walked over to the Police Scotland officers. He shook the hand of firearms officer Sergeant Jamie Miles.

'Long time, no see, Jamie,' he said. 'Thanks for the help.'

'No problem. They give you any trouble?'

'Rory pulled a knife on me.'

'I told you to be careful,' said Miles. 'The man's a psycho. Do you want us to arrest him?'

'No, it would only make things worse. Angus told him to put it away after he saw you anyway.'

'Wise boy,' said Miles. 'Do you think they killed her then?'

'That remains to be seen,' said Harris. He turned towards the Land Rover.

'Well, let me know if you need anything else,' said Miles. 'Safe journey back, guys.'

Gallagher did not speak until the Land Rover was bumping its way down the track towards the main road. Eventually, as the inspector turned the vehicle onto the eastbound carriageway of the A75, the sergeant could contain himself no longer.

'Safe journey back!' he exclaimed angrily and glared at Harris. 'We're lucky we are going back. Alan Jay's right, you push it too far, sometimes. What happened back there was reckless. Rory could have killed you.'

'Only in his dreams,' said Harris.

'The bastard pulled a knife on you, for God's sake!'

'Yes, but he wouldn't have got the chance to use it.'

'Yes, well, I've said my bit,' said Gallagher. 'Much good may it do me.'

An uneasy silence settled on the vehicle for a few moments. As usual, it was broken by Gallagher.

'What do you think, anyway?' he asked. 'Do you think they had anything to do with Rosie's death?'

'I think that our esteemed professor is becoming ever more interesting,' said Harris.

Chapter fifteen

Alison Butterfield and Sally Orr drove the half hour from Levton Bridge to the village of Amberthorpe and headed for the end of the main street, as instructed by Betty Lord. Butterfield knocked on the front door of a small white cottage with an immaculate front garden. The door was opened by a white-haired woman wearing a green cardigan and tweed skirt. She greeted them with a welcoming smile.

'Betty Lord?' asked the constable.

'Yes, and you must be Detective Constables Butterfield and Orr,' said the woman. 'I hope you do not think me rude, but can I see your warrant cards, please? I've seen enough episodes of *Midsomer Murders* to know that you can't be too careful.'

'And you're right to ask,' said Butterfield. The officers held their cards up so that Betty could see.

Five minutes later, they were seated in the living room, whose walls were adorned with numerous photographs of wildflowers. The officers were sipping tea out of floral-decorated bone china cups and munching appreciatively on lemon drizzle cake.

'This is delicious,' said Butterfield. 'Did you make it yourself?'

'I did indeed.'

'You didn't need to go to all this trouble.'

'It's not every day that one becomes involved in a homicide investigation,' said Betty. The word seemed incongruous coming out of such a genteel woman's mouth and, noticing the officers' surprise, Betty chuckled. 'I watch a lot of episodes of *Law and Order* in the afternoon as well. The Americans refer to murders as homicides, as I am sure you know.'

The constables smiled; there was something instantly likeable about the pensioner.

'So,' said Betty, looking at Butterfield, 'from what you said on the phone, I gather that you want to know about Professor Nesbitt in relation to the death of that poor woman? Can I ask if he is a suspect?'

'It's far too early to say,' said Butterfield. Recalling Gallagher's constant reminders to think before speaking, she chose her next words carefully. 'However, what I can say is that he is of interest to our inquiry.'

'Do you know who she was?' asked Betty. 'The radio didn't name her and Ross was very mysterious when I asked him.'

'We have not released the name yet,' said Butterfield.

Betty shook her head.

'You have to feel for the family, don't you?' she said.

Butterfield and Orr thought of all the things they had heard about the Grogans and did not comment.

'Tell me about Gordon Nesbitt,' said Butterfield instead. 'You met him thirty years ago, I think, but he did not make a good impression on you?'

'No, he didn't,' said Betty. 'It sounds an awful thing to say but I'm not entirely surprised that he is mixed up in something like this. As I told Ross, he was creepy.'

'Yes, what did you mean by that?' asked Orr.

'Like he was always eyeing the women up. And a couple of them said that he brushed up against them.'

Betty frowned. 'No, there was something about the man that none of us liked.'

'How many times did you meet him?' asked Orr.

'A couple of times that summer. We took him to a few of the sites we had been studying. He used the information for articles he was writing. He became quite an authority on the subject, did Gordon.'

'Did you take him to Meadowview House?' asked Orr.

'No. George Stillwell had no time for visitors and he had been extremely unpleasant when the group asked if we could document the wildflowers on his land so we stayed away.'

'Do you think Professor Nesbitt went there anyway?' asked Butterfield.

'I know he did.' Betty gestured to the cake. 'Would either of you like some more?'

The constables both nodded and, after serving the slices, Betty continued with her story.

'Gordon said he thought that George was going to chase him off the first time he visited the house,' she said. 'The old man was pretty angry, apparently. However, although George would not let him in the house, Gordon did eventually persuade him to let him go onto the meadows. Goodness knows how he did it. It's more than we ever got out of the old curmudgeon. We had to look down on them from outside George's land.'

'Was the professor alone when he visited the valley?' asked Orr.

'He was when we saw him. The first thing I knew about the young girl was when it was on the radio.'

'Did Professor Nesbitt ever mention bringing students up here?' asked Orr.

'No, he didn't,' said Betty. 'And you'd think he would, wouldn't you?'

'Not if he didn't want anyone to know,' said Butterfield.

Silence settled on the room; it was a troubling thought.

***

The growing belief that the professor was a strong suspect was one that the constables took into the briefing that was held at Levton Bridge Police Station later that afternoon when Harris and Gallagher had returned from Scotland. Harris stood in front of a noticeboard that was now much more populated than previously.

'So,' said the inspector. He tapped the image of Rosie Grogan that had been pinned up in the centre of the board. 'We now know that our victim had connections to several people in whom we are interested.'

He ran his hand across to mugshots of Davie Grogan and his sons, which had been supplied by Police Scotland from their arrests in 2005.

'We know that the Grogans did not like the fact that Rosie persisted with her studies despite Davie telling her not to,' he said. 'And we know that the situation was causing them to lose face. In the Grogans' world, that's a big deal.'

'Maybe so but, if you ask me, Professor Nesbitt is a much better suspect,' said Gillian Roberts.

'Convince me,' said Harris.

'We know that Rosie attended the Institute of Botany when Nesbitt worked there, we know that he had visited Meadowview House and we know that he was creepy around women.' Roberts looked at Butterfield and Orr, who nodded their agreement. 'What's more, he'd have known that the house was standing empty. Maybe he took Rosie there, tried it on with her and things went badly wrong.'

'Yes, but why leave the body?' asked Alistair Marshall. 'If he'd buried her up on the hills, she would probably never have been found. He must have known that somebody would buy the house one day.'

'Perhaps he thought that it would be difficult to identify her,' said Roberts. 'DNA wasn't very well known in those days, remember. And even if she was found, perhaps he hoped that fingers would point at Old Man Stillwell. After all, who else could it be and who would suspect a much-respected professor with a thing for flowers, anyway?'

'Trouble is,' said Harris, 'there's not a shred of proof to back up your suspicions, Gillian. That's why I want Matty to visit him in London tomorrow. Take Sally with you. It'll be good experience.'

Orr beamed at being given the opportunity to take centre stage in a murder inquiry. Butterfield looked disappointed but said nothing.

'You not fancy going yourself?' asked Gallagher.

'I have to be here,' said Harris. 'The Press Office is going to release Rosie's name first thing in the morning and they're expecting a lot of media interest.'

Gallagher appeared about to say something but thought twice about it.

'Go on,' said Harris. 'What's on your mind?'

Gallagher hesitated; it felt like he had spent a lot of time treading on eggshells in his dealings with Harris over recent days.

'All I was going to say is that there's someone missing from the board,' said the sergeant. He was choosing his words carefully. 'Someone who knew that the house was empty and who was also knocking about with the Grogans at the time Rosie vanished.'

'My old pal John Foster,' said Harris.

'I'm not saying he was involved,' said Gallagher, relieved that the inspector had taken the suggestion the right way. 'But I don't think we can discount him. Not yet anyway.'

'And you're right.' Harris looked at Butterfield, who was struggling to conceal her disappointment at being overlooked for the London trip. 'Which is why you can get rid of the pet lip, Alison. I want you and Alistair to work the gangland angle.'

'Brilliant!' exclaimed Butterfield.

'You'd not be so enthusiastic if you'd met the Grogans,' said Gallagher sourly, recalling the sight of the knife in Rory's hand.

'She won't meet them,' said Harris. 'The Organised Crime guys in Glasgow have tracked down an old intelligence report on Rosie's disappearance and I have arranged for us to meet a couple of their people to pick it up.'

Chapter sixteen

As Butterfield and Marshall were setting off for a motorway service station on the M74 in Scotland the next morning, Gallagher and Orr were heading south on a train to London. Having arrived in the capital, they took a black cab to the residential home where Gordon Nesbitt lived. As the car headed up the drive towards the converted Victorian villa, Orr's eyes gleamed; she was relishing the experience, having only once previously been to London and that on a weekend away with her parents when she was a teenager. Noticing her eagerness. Gallagher chuckled.

'Bit better than trying to find your graffiti artist, eh?' he said.

'Just a bit,' said the constable as the vehicle pulled up outside the home.

Once the officers had signed in at reception, a member of staff ushered them towards a small lounge off one of the corridors. Before entering the room, the detectives stood in silence and stared through the glass panel in the door at the frail white-haired man sitting in one of the armchairs.

'He doesn't look like a murderer,' whispered Orr.

'Think of him thirty years ago,' said Gallagher. 'When he was fitter and stronger. What was he capable of doing when he was like that?'

The sergeant pushed open the door and Gordon Nesbitt gave them a welcoming smile and gestured to the walking stick propped up against the armchair.

'Please forgive me if I don't get up,' he said. 'I'm not too good on my feet these days.'

'That's fine,' said Gallagher.

The officers showed the professor their warrant cards then dragged chairs across and sat down. Both were struck by how unconcerned he appeared at their presence in the room. Perhaps, they thought, they had the wrong man – which was when the professor glanced at Orr.

'You are most welcome, my dear,' he said. There was a glint in his eye. 'Pretty young women always are, even at my age.'

A chill ran down the constable's spine as she recalled the sergeant's words of a few moments before. *Think of him thirty years ago. When he was fitter and stronger. What was he capable of doing when he was like that?* She looked at Gallagher, who raised an eyebrow ever so slightly. If Nesbitt noticed the gesture, he did not show it.

'So, what's this about?' asked the professor. Despite his frail appearance, the voice was strong. 'The matron wouldn't tell me why you have travelled all this way to see me.'

'Are you aware of what has been happening at Meadowview House?' asked Gallagher.

'Yes, it's very gratifying.'

The detectives exchanged bemused glances.

'Gratifying?' said Gallagher.

'Yes. The plan for a visitor centre sounds excellent. I always said that someone should do something to preserve the site once the old man died. The meadows are very precious. But why would the police be interested, though?'

'Because of the discovery of a body under the floorboards,' said the sergeant slowly.

The old man stared at him in astonishment.

'A body?' he said.

'You didn't know?' said Gallagher. 'It's been all over the news.'

'I'm afraid I do not take much interest in the news,' said Nesbitt. 'I don't watch television or read newspapers and I'm not on the Internet. Never have been. Don't understand it.'

'So how do you know about the plan for the visitor centre then?'

'There was an article in *British Wildlife* magazine a few months back when it was first announced.' The professor frowned. 'But why would you want to talk to me about a body? I know nothing about that. Who was it?'

'A student called Rosie Grogan,' said Gallagher.

If the detectives were hoping for a self-incriminating reaction from Nesbitt, they were to be disappointed as the professor's expression was impassive and without a flicker of recognition.

'Rosie Grogan,' murmured Nesbitt. He furrowed his brows. 'Rosie Grogan. The name does not ring a bell.'

'She was one of your students at the Henderson Institute of Botany,' said Gallagher. He produced a copy of the photograph of Rosie. 'This is her.'

The professor studied the picture for a few moments then shook his head.

'I'm sorry, I don't recognise her,' said the professor. 'But then there were so many students over the years and, after a while, young people all look the same to us old 'uns, even the pretty ones like her.'

The professor winked at Orr, who felt a tight knot forming in her stomach.

'She was from Glasgow,' said Gallagher. He placed the picture on a side table next to the professor's chair. 'Are you sure you don't remember her? Her family didn't approve of her studying botany.'

'Now I come to think of it, there was a student like that,' said Nesbitt. He looked at the picture again, more closely this time. 'Yes, it could be her. As I recall, it was assumed at the time she left that she had dropped out of her course. Quite a lot of them did.'

'We are wondering if you ever took her to see Meadowview House?' asked Gallagher. 'Just you and her? On the day that this picture was taken, perhaps? Maybe you took it?'

The old man looked shocked at the suggestion.

'Oh, no,' he said with a vigorous shake of the head. 'That would have been against the rules. The Institute was very strict when it came to lecturers consorting with students. I think I'd have remembered if I'd done something like that, don't you? How did the poor young girl die?'

'She was murdered.'

'How terrible. And with so much of her life ahead of her.' Nesbitt gave Gallagher a sharp look. 'But, surely, I am not a suspect?'

'We've been told that you visited the area several times around the time she vanished and that you went to Meadowview House on at least one occasion,' said Gallagher.

'Who told you that?' asked Nesbitt. His voice had changed. He was more guarded now. 'The women from the botany group have been gossiping, I suppose.'

'Who told us is not important, Professor. What is important is that we know that when Rosie went to Meadowview House, she had someone else with her and we think it might have been you. We know that you wrote articles about the place.'

'You've read my work?' asked Nesbitt. He seemed pleased. 'How gratifying. You are right, I went to

Meadowview House twice as part of my research but I went alone on both occasions.'

'Did you...?' began Gallagher.

Nesbitt closed his eyes.

'I'm sorry,' he said, 'but I'm very tired. I wonder if you could go now, please?'

'But we want to ask you some more questions.'

'I really am very tired,' said Nesbitt. He did not open his eyes. 'It's the illness, you know. However, I can assure you that I know nothing about young Rosie Grogan.'

The detectives watched him for a couple of moments, wondering if he'd gone to sleep, then Gallagher shrugged at Orr and they headed for the door. They were just about to leave the room when Nesbitt spoke again.

'You'd be better off asking Geoffrey about Meadowview House instead of talking to me,' he said. 'He seemed very interested in the place.'

Gallagher stared at him.

'Geoffrey?' he said.

The old man opened his eyes.

'Yes,' he said. 'I think his surname is Haynes. He's one of the visitors that the local church sends to keep us old fogeys company, although I haven't seen him for a while. He was very interested when I showed him the article about Meadowview House in the magazine. He asked me a lot of questions.'

'Like what?' asked Gallagher.

The professor closed his eyes again and it was clear that the conversation was at an end. Having left the room, the officers sought out the manager of the home, who was in her office.

'We haven't seen Mr Haynes for several months,' she said in response to Gallagher's query.

'Why's that?' asked the sergeant.

'I rang the church about him after he missed a couple of appointments but they said that they hadn't heard from him either, so they assumed that he'd stopped visiting people. It happens all the time. It's all very well using volunteers but not all of them are reliable, I am afraid.'

A couple of minutes later, the detectives were walking back down the drive towards the main road where they hoped to hail another taxi.

'So, what do you think?' asked Orr.

'I think that Gordon Nesbitt knows more than he is letting on,' said the sergeant.

'I agree. And now I know what Betty Lord meant when she said that he was creepy. I felt the same. Did you see the way that he looked at me?'

'I did, yes.'

'So do you think he killed Rosie?' asked Orr as they reached the bottom of the drive. 'Should we not go back and arrest him?'

'On what grounds? That he gave you a funny look? No, we need more evidence before we go round arresting frail old men. Harris said that we could only bring him in if we were one hundred per cent sure and, let's be honest about it, Sally, we're not, are we?'

Orr shook her head and Gallagher spotted a cab and stuck out his hand.

'Come on,' he said as the vehicle slowed to a halt. 'I said that we'd grab a cuppa with my pal in the CID before we headed back. Thank him for his help and see if he's got anything else on Haynes.'

'At least we know where he found out about Meadowview House,' said Orr as they clambered into the taxi. 'It's a small world, isn't it?'

Chapter seventeen

Alison Butterfield could not conceal her excitement as Alistair Marshall guided his car up the slip road leading off the M74 and into the motorway services where they were to meet the detectives from the Glasgow Organised Crime Unit.

'This is more like it,' she said. Her eyes were gleaming. 'Better than chasing some kid with a spray can.'

'Yes, well just watch what you say in there,' said Marshall as he parked the car and turned off the engine. 'We don't know how much of it will get back to the Grogans.'

'Why should it?'

'I'm just passing on what Harris said to me before we left,' replied Marshall. He locked the car. 'He said that you have to trust no one when it comes to organised crime.'

Five minutes later, the two officers were sitting drinking tea at a corner table in the coffee shop on the main concourse when they were approached by a man and a woman, both in their late forties. The man was carrying a tray bearing hot drinks and a couple of pieces of cake. He looked the Levton Bridge detectives up and down, raised an eyebrow and glanced at his colleague.

'I must be getting old,' he said. 'Police officers are looking younger and younger these days.'

The woman gave a slight smile and Marshall, noting that Butterfield had opened her mouth to retort, gave her a warning look. Butterfield closed her mouth.

The Glasgow detectives sat down and, introductions having been made, Detective Sergeant Graham Leonard glanced round to make sure that they were not being watched by people at neighbouring tables. Satisfied, he slid a brown A4 Manilla envelope across the table.

'That's a copy of the intelligence report your governor wanted,' he said.

'God knows how it survived this long,' said his colleague, Detective Constable Mary Ballard. 'The office has been redecorated three times.'

'Have you read it?' asked Marshall.

'I have and it's pretty thin stuff,' said Leonard. 'Mostly unsubstantiated rumour suggesting that a rival gang did for young Rosie.'

'The guys working organised crime at the time had their money on her being in the concrete foundations of one of the new office blocks down by the river,' said Ballard. 'The Grogans certainly believed that's what had happened to her.'

'How do you know that?' asked Butterfield.

'The report says that an informant was in the same pub as Angus not long after Rosie disappeared,' said Ballard. 'He overheard Angus say that he knew who had taken her but couldn't prove it. Apparently, he said that he wasn't going to name him for fear of sparking a full-scale turf war. The discovery that he was wrong has clearly got the Grogans rattled.'

'How so?' asked Marshall.

'The moment your guys left Davie's house after telling him that Rosie had been found, Angus and Rory hightailed it back to Glasgow and started putting themselves about, trying to find out what people had been saying about them. Your governor's mate John Foster got a real grilling once the Grogans realised they were old pals. Now, Foster has gone to ground. The word is that he's left the city.'

'So, do you think the Grogans were behind Rosie's death?' asked Butterfield.

'Not sure,' said Ballard. 'And there's no way they would admit it, even if they were.'

'Well, we're going to find out, whether they like it or not,' said Butterfield.

'Is that right?' said Ballard with a slight smile as she noted that the young officer was unable to contain her excitement. 'Well, it's all very well being enthusiastic, Constable, but you'd do well not to underestimate the Grogans. This isn't a game, you know.'

'Yes, but they are yesterday's men, aren't they?' said Butterfield. 'I mean, they're past it, aren't they?'

Her voice was louder than she had meant and one or two people at nearby tables glanced in the detectives' direction. Leonard gave Butterfield a sharp look.

'Keep your bloody voice down,' he said. 'And, whatever you do, don't go round suggesting that the Grogans are past it. Rory went for your governor with a knife, remember. Davie may be an old man but he's perfectly capable of ordering Rory to slash a copper if he thinks they're getting too close. Glasgow is not like the sticks, young lady. You're playing with the big boys now.'

The Glasgow detectives stood up to leave and Leonard tapped the envelope, which was still lying on the table.

'Don't lose it,' he said.

As the two detectives headed off across the concourse, Butterfield and Marshall watched them with glum expressions on their faces; they could see that they were laughing. The Levton Bridge officers gave their Scottish counterparts a few minutes to leave the service station before walking across the car park and getting into Marshall's vehicle. Butterfield put her seatbelt on and looked across at her colleague.

'I made a fool of myself, didn't I?' she said gloomily. She was acutely aware that the older officers had addressed her as if she was a rookie on her first day on the job. 'Got a bit carried away?'

'A bit, maybe, but they were well out of order.'

'You'd think that a female officer would afford another female officer some respect, though.'

'I'd forget it, if I were you,' said Marshall. He reversed the vehicle out of its parking space.

'Do you think the Grogans really would go after a cop?' asked Butterfield. Concern had replaced embarrassment and the constable felt a tight knot in her stomach. 'I mean, Rory did pull a knife on the governor, didn't he?'

'He did but, if you ask me, those two back there were laying it on thick. Playing the Big I Ams to impress the country bumpkins. I wouldn't worry about it.'

'I'm not worried,' said Butterfield. She tried to look relaxed.

'You sure?' said Marshall. He glanced across at her. 'You look a bit pale. I did try to warn you.'

'I'm fine,' said Butterfield.

However, she didn't relax until their vehicle was several miles from the services, heading south as the M74 cut through forested hills. Only then did she slide the intelligence report out of the envelope, scan the contents and ring Jack Harris.

* * *

Having spent the morning giving interviews, the inspector was taking the dogs for a walk round the park near the police station when his mobile phone rang. He pulled the mobile out of his coat pocket, glanced at the readout and gave a knowing smile. He unclipped the dogs' leads so the animals could run free and sat down on a bench to take the call.

'Alison,' he said. 'How goes it?'

'We've just left the services.'

'And did the meeting go well?' asked the inspector as he watched the dogs running across the grass.

Something in her boss's voice alerted Butterfield's suspicions.

'You know it didn't, don't you?' she said.

'Yeah. Graham Leonard rang me.'

'He didn't hang around. Am I in trouble?'

'No, you're not,' said Harris. He thought about his unguarded comment about John Foster to the Grogans. 'However, I would have thought that you'd have learned by now that you have to be careful with grizzled old lags like those two. And me, for that matter. A lot of us older cops forget that we were young once.'

'I'll try,' said Butterfield, overwhelmed by a sense of relief that she had not fallen foul of the inspector.

'Now,' said Harris. 'You've got the intelligence report, I think? Any use?'

'It doesn't add much to what we know already.' Butterfield tried to sound professional as she glanced at the two pages of A4 on her lap. 'Everyone seemed to think that Rosie was kidnapped by a rival gang. The Grogans were engaged in a whole series of turf wars over heroin and folks thought it was tied up with that.'

'Does the report name John Foster?' asked Harris.

Noting that Scoot was about to do his business on the bowls green, the inspector stood up and walked quickly towards the animal. 'Hey! Off there! The club president will have my guts for garters if he sees you doing that. Sorry, Alison, you were about to tell me about John Foster.'

'He's not mentioned but the Grogans have been giving him a hard time, apparently. Trying to find out his relationship with you. He seems to have gone to ground.'

'I don't blame him.'

Butterfield was surprised to hear her boss give a low chuckle.

'What's so funny?' she asked.

'I've just seen the latest graffiti on the bowls club's pavilion. I'm not sure the parish council chairman can do that, not at his age and certainly not with his bad back. You'd best get back to finding Boz when you return. I've no doubt that the chairman will be bending the commander's ear about it, as we speak.'

'But I thought that I was supposed to be focusing on the gangs,' said Butterfield. She was unable to conceal the disappointment in her voice.

'Yes, well I want you to come up with something to tell Curtis about the graffiti first. The vagaries of police work, I am afraid, Constable. See you when you get back.'

On reaching the park gates, the inspector put the dogs on their leads and headed back towards the police station. He was walking up the hill leading to the marketplace when he saw a familiar figure standing at the bottom of the steps outside the police station.

'Well, well, well,' murmured the inspector. 'I wonder what he could possibly want?'

The man turned to face him as the inspector approached.

'Long time, no see,' said Harris. 'And now I can't get away from you.'

'You can forget the fucking pleasantries,' said John Foster angrily. He jabbed a finger at his old friend. 'What have you been saying to the Grogans about me?'

Chapter eighteen

John Foster had calmed down a little by the time Harris had settled him in the interview room next to the police station's reception area and given him a mug of tea with his usual two sugars. Sitting down opposite his old friend at the table, Harris noted that he looked tired and nervous and had not shaved for a couple of days. The inspector's mind went back thirty years to the fresh-faced, bright-eyed teenager with whom he roamed the hills on long summer days and he was filled with an overwhelming sense of the passage of time, as he had been on numerous occasions during the investigation.

The major reason that Foster had started to relax was down to the presence of the dogs in the room. Harris knew that he had always loved dogs and had rarely been without them during their teenage years growing up in the valley.

'You still got one?' asked Harris, nodding towards Scoot and Archie.

'I used to,' said Foster sadly. 'But we live on a busy road and my last one got run over a couple of years ago so I decided not to risk it after that. I was gutted. So were the kids.'

'I bet they were. How many children have you got?'

'Two,' said Foster. 'Both boys. Fifteen and twelve. You?'

'No.'

'I'm not surprised,' said Foster. 'They were never going to be your thing, were they?'

'Not really,' said Harris. He did not mention that the subject had cropped up in conversation with his girlfriend. The inspector had resolved to regard his old friend with circumspection until he was certain that he could trust him.

Foster ruffled the fur on Scoot's head.

'I miss having a dog something rotten, mind,' he said.

'I'm sure you do,' said Harris. He looked intently at his old friend. 'But you didn't come here to talk about dogs, did you? What brought you to Levton Bridge?'

Foster scowled.

'You and your big mouth, that's what,' he said. 'I could have done without you telling Angus that you and me go way back.'

'That's all I said,' replied Harris. 'Nothing more. I'm sorry, I wasn't thinking.'

'Yeah, well whatever you said, it was enough. Any friend of the police is no friend of the Grogans and Angus has got it into his head that I'm the one that told you they killed Rosie. I had to do some fast talking to persuade him otherwise, I can tell you.'

'Well, they didn't get it from me,' said Harris. 'Did they did kill her, do you think?'

'They may have been capable of many things in those days — they were crazy times — but killing their own flesh and blood?' Foster shook his head. 'No, I can't see it, Hawk. The old man was genuinely devastated when Rosie vanished and really upset when you told him that she'd been found. He always hoped that she was still alive somewhere.'

'You seem to be very close to the family,' said Harris. 'How come you got mixed up with them in the first place?'

'Don't get the wrong idea about me. I've never been involved in any of their gangland activities.' Foster noticed his friend's sceptical expression. 'I admit that I knocked around with some of their associates when I was much younger but I was never into organised crime.'

'Then how come the local police think that you have been laundering money for the Grogans?' Harris took a sip of tea and grimaced when he realised that it had gone cold. 'You have to admit that takes some explaining.'

'It's not what it looks like. It's the local cops trying anything they can to stir up trouble. Angus and Rory have been among my best customers for years. Anyway, a few years back, the business ran into cash flow problems and it looked like I might have to close. Angus offered to bail me out in return for a share of the profits. That's all there is to it. A straightforward business deal.'

'Yet you were close enough to the Grogans to tip them off about me and Matty Gallagher meeting Malcom Gray in the coffee shop,' said Harris.

'I admit that I pass on bits of information from time to time,' said Foster. 'It keeps me in their good books and they'd have heard from someone else, anyway. Everyone knows what happened in Manchester so you coming to Glasgow is big news. I hadn't reckoned on you telling them that we were old buddies, though. Rory was itching to have a go and you know what he's like. I heard that he went for you with a knife?'

'Grief can do strange things to a person,' said Harris with a deadpan look.

'This isn't something to be taken lightly. The man's always been a headcase, you know that. You need to be careful.'

'I could have taken him,' said Harris. 'I was taught self-defence by SAS instructors when I was in the Army. He wouldn't have stood a chance.'

'Same old Jack Harris,' said Foster with a slight smile. 'Thinks he's invincible.'

'Too true,' said the inspector. 'Look, if you're here to ask for protection from the Grogans, I'm not sure I can help. My budget is stretched as it is. Besides there're some folks see you as a suspect for Rosie's death because you knew about Meadowview House being empty.'

'I had nothing to do with what happened to her!' exclaimed Foster. He seemed genuinely aghast at the suggestion. 'However, I am looking to do a deal with you. Information in return for you getting the Grogans off my back.'

'I'm listening,' said Harris.

'When Rosie's body turned up, Angus started saying that maybe she was killed by someone who took her to see the meadows. He started saying that maybe she went with someone from the place where she had been studying. I'd been thinking the same. Angus has been trying to find out who it might have been.'

'Has he now?' said Harris. He tried to appear casual, unconcerned, as if the information was of little importance, but the inspector was alarmed at the thought that both he and the Grogans were honing in on the professor. 'Did he mention anyone in particular?'

'Not to me but I thought you'd like to know. In return, I want you to tell the Grogans that the rumours that I have been talking to you are not true.'

Harris thought for a few moments and nodded.

'Fair enough,' he said.

'Thank you,' said Foster. He stood up. 'Now, assuming that you do not plan to arrest me for anything, I'll be off.'

'Are you going back to Glasgow?'

'I'm going to stay up here for a few days,' said Foster. 'The last thing I want is to be in Glasgow with the Grogans on the warpath. I'll stay with my mum over at Carpbery. It's ages since I've been to see her, anyway.'

'Give her my regards,' said Harris. 'I still bump into her from time to time when she comes into town on market day. She's looking well.'

'Yeah, not bad for eighty-one. I'll tell her you were asking after her.' Foster gave a smile. 'And it's good to see you after all these years, Hawk. I just wish that the circumstances could have been different.'

'Yeah, me too,' said Harris.

Foster opened the door and stepped into the reception area.

'John,' said Harris.

Foster turned back and noticed that the inspector was holding out one of his business cards. He hesitated.

'Take it,' said Harris. 'You never know when you may need me.'

Foster nodded and slipped the card into his back trouser pocket.

'Don't bank on it, though,' he said. 'You're bad news.'

* * *

After Foster had left the police station, a pensive Harris was walking along the corridor on his way to see the commander when his mobile phone rang. He leaned against a windowsill to take the call.

'Matty lad,' he said. 'Just the person. Have you seen the professor yet?'

'Sure have.'

'And?'

'We reckon there's more to him than a fusty old academic, but we followed your instructions not to go in too heavy. He's pretty frail. Interestingly, it turns out that Geoffrey Haynes used to visit him for the local church, which is where he heard about Meadowview House.'

'Which explains why he suddenly appeared on the scene.' The inspector could hear an engine in the background. 'Where are you now?'

'In a taxi heading for the railway station.'

Harris was silent for a few moments as he looked out of the window and noticed Alan Jay walking across the yard towards the back door. Clearly, the man was still stirring things.

'You still there?' asked Gallagher.

'Yeah, sorry. Listen, don't get on a train just yet. I might want you to bring Nesbitt up here. John Foster reckons that the Grogans have worked out that Rosie might have been killed by someone at the Institute. If we can find the professor, so can they.'

'Jesus, that did not take long,' said Gallagher. The concern was clear in his voice. 'When did he tell you this then?'

'Just now. He came to see me.'

'We'll get back to the home then,' said Gallagher.

'Yeah, do that but don't move in until I tell you,' said Harris. 'I want to talk to the CPS before we do anything. Arresting frail old men can be what our beloved commander likes to call a "PR disaster" if we get it wrong.'

* * *

The conversation at an end, Harris resumed his progress towards the commander's office where Curtis gestured for him to take a seat.

'How's it going?' asked the commander.

'Pretty well,' said Harris. 'You might be interested to know that my old mate John Foster has just been in to give us some useful information.'

'I hope that you saw him in the company of another officer.'

'No, just me.'

'Well, make sure that you make a full record of the meeting,' said the commander. 'I don't want us giving Alan Jay any ammunition to use against you. We play this one by the book, yes?'

'There's a book?' said Harris innocently.

Curtis gave him a withering look, but Harris could tell that he had enjoyed the comment. The inspector gave the commander an impish smile.

'Talking of the interim head of the Professional Standards Unit,' he said, 'will you tell him that he was wrong to suggest taking me off the inquiry, or should I?'

'No, I'll do it,' said Curtis.

'It's just that I've just seen him in the yard. Should I go and find him for you?'

Curtis gave a slight smile.

'You really are your own worst enemy,' he said.

Chapter nineteen

'I must say, it's a red-letter day when Jack Harris asks for the CPS's advice on making an arrest,' said the lawyer. Jane Malham looked across the desk at the inspector and gave a wry smile. 'Alan Jay will be delighted to hear that his drive for better professional standards has had such an instantaneous an effect on you. I had a meeting with him yesterday and he had an awful lot to say about the way you operate.'

'You can go off someone very quickly, you know,' said Harris.

Malham chuckled. She and Harris were sitting in the commander's office and Philip Curtis allowed himself a slight smile as he observed the banter between the two of them. Malham glanced at the commander.

'Sorry, sir,' said Malham. 'Couldn't resist it.'

'No need to apologise,' said Curtis. 'However, I also have a meeting with the sainted Alan in ten minutes so can we get on with it, please?'

'Of course, sir. Sorry.' Malham turned back to Harris. 'What's your main concern, Jack?'

'That the evidence against Professor Nesbitt is very thin and if I tell Matty to bring him in for questioning, I am opening the force up to a charge of wrongful arrest. Also, if we are wrong, the media will have a field day. He's a very sick old man.'

'Age has nothing to do with it,' said Malham. 'If you're suspected of committing a crime, you should have to explain yourself, however old you are. Look at the elderly Nazis that they still bring before the courts. You should treat Nesbitt like any other suspect, Jack. However, from what you've told me, I agree that what you have *is* thin and a good solicitor will pull it apart. Do you have anything else on Nesbitt, apart from the fact that some old dear thinks that he was creepy?'

'I am afraid not,' replied Harris. 'He's not got a record, there's no soft intelligence on him and the events happened thirty years ago without any witnesses that we know of.'

'So, given that we don't have enough cause to justify an arrest, we're snookered if he refuses to come voluntarily, aren't we?' said Curtis.

'Unless we take him into protective custody on the grounds that the Grogans may be after him,' said Harris.

'But we don't know that they are, do we?' said Curtis. 'All we have is John Foster's word for it and, even then, we don't know if the Grogans know about the professor, do we? I'd need an awful lot more to justify the expenditure on protective custody with the way budgets are, Jack.'

The inspector's mobile phone rang.

'Hopefully, this is good news,' said Harris and took the call. 'Sally, what you got?'

'My contact at the University of South East London has just rang me,' said Orr. The constable sounded worried. 'Apparently, they've had someone in asking questions about any field trips that Rosie might have made when she was at the Henderson Institute.'

'Do they know who it was?'

'He wouldn't give his name but you'd guess that it was someone who knows the Grogans,' said Orr. 'He left in a hurry when a member of staff challenged him.'

'Did anyone give him Professor Nesbitt's name?'

'Not as far as we can tell. My contact has also managed to track down one of the former staff at the Institute. The sarge's pal down here has arranged for officers to keep an eye on the home so we're on our way to see her.'

'Keep me posted,' said Harris. He ended the call and looked at Curtis and Malham with a grim expression on his face. 'It would seem that the Grogans may be closing in on the professor.'

'Are you going to bring him in then?' asked Malham.

'Maybe,' said Harris. He stood up. 'But I want to see what Matty and Sally turn up first.'

Harris had just left the commander's office when he saw Alan Jay walking towards him along the corridor,

'Ah, Alan,' said the inspector affably. 'Just the man. I've just been in with the CPS discussing a possible arrest on the Meadowview House case. It's a delicate one and we do like to follow the correct procedures. Thought you'd like to know.'

The inspector strode back towards his office, whistling as he went, watched by a glowering Alan Jay.

* * *

Back in London, Gallagher and Orr got out of the taxi at the end of a row of terraced houses in Southwark. The constable glanced at the note in her hand.

'Number 24,' she said. 'The one with the green door.'

The detectives walked up to the property and Gallagher rang the bell. The door was opened by a grey-haired woman, who walked with the aid of a stick.

'Gail Ronson?' asked Gallagher. 'Police.'

The detectives held up their warrant cards and, when she had read them, Gail Ronson stood aside to let them enter the house.

'Anna said you might want to talk to me,' she said as she led them into the living room, the walls of which were adorned with photographs of flowers. 'It must be important for you to come all this way. Is Professor Nesbitt in trouble?'

'He might be,' said Gallagher as he and Orr sat down on the sofa. 'Suffice to say that it's a murder inquiry.'

Gail Ronson looked shocked.

'Well, of course I'll help you in any way that I can,' she said. 'Would you like a cup of tea before we start?'

The detectives nodded and she disappeared into the kitchen from where they could hear the clink of cups and saucers. She re-emerged a few minutes later, poured out the drinks and handed round a plate of biscuits then settled down in an armchair.

'Now,' she said. 'You said that it's a murder inquiry. Is Gordon a suspect?'

'He's certainly someone who may have useful information,' said Gallagher. He reached for a biscuit.

'I'm not sure I can be of much assistance,' said Ronson. 'I haven't seen Gordon Nesbitt for the best part of thirty years.'

'It happened round about that time,' said Gallagher. 'We are investigating the death of a young student from the Institute, whose body was found beneath the floorboards of a house in the North Pennines, a house that we know Professor Nesbitt visited on a number of occasions. You might have heard about it on the news? Meadowview House?'

'I don't really follow the news these days.' Gail Ronson hesitated. 'However, there was always the danger that something like this would happen.'

The detectives exchanged glances.

'What do you mean?' asked Gallagher.

'Gordon had been warned about taking students on field trips without clearing it with the Board. It was against the Institute's guidelines but he thought that the rules did not apply to him. He's that kind of man. Very arrogant.'

'How many times did he do it?' asked Orr.

'I'm not sure. Four or five, maybe. I don't remember the students' names, I am afraid.'

'Always young women, though?' asked the constable.

'I am afraid so. He would warn them not to tell anyone about it because they might be expelled from the course but then it all came out when one of them told another lecturer. What was the name of the student who died?'

'Rosie Grogan,' said Gallagher.

'Blonde?'

'You knew her?' said the sergeant.

'I knew Gordon's type.'

Gallagher produced the copy of the photograph taken at Meadowview House from his pocket and held it up.

'Was she one of the ones that Gordon took on a field trip?' he asked.

'I'm sorry, I don't recall. It was thirty years ago but I do remember her, however. Scottish?'

'That's her,' said Gallagher.

'Such a nice girl. I often wondered what happened to her after she dropped out of the course.'

'Did you not wonder why she did that?' asked Gallagher.

'Students dropped out all the time. I seem to recall that her family were very strongly opposed to her continuing her studies, particularly her father. I just assumed that he had forced her to leave. He came with one of his sons to clear out her room and they didn't seem to be particularly pleasant people.'

'That's something of an understatement,' said Gallagher. 'Tell me, was there ever any suggestion that Gordon acted inappropriately with the women he took on field trips?'

'Not that I heard.' Gail frowned. 'However, and perhaps I shouldn't say this, there was always something disturbing about the way he was around women. The way he looked at them.'

'In what way?' asked Orr.

'Creepy.'

Gallagher and Orr exchanged glances. That word again. Once the interview was at an end and they were back in the street, the sergeant rang Harris. After the conversation had ended, Harris walked into the CPS office where Jane Malham looked up from the document she was reading.

'I don't think that we'll need protective custody to justify arresting the professor,' said the inspector. 'He seems to have taken a number of young women on unauthorised field trips and intimidated them into not telling anyone.'

'You'd best bring him in then,' said the lawyer.

Chapter twenty

Gallagher and Orr stayed overnight in London, having made arrangements for the professor to be taken into custody the following morning. They arrived at the home courtesy of a car and driver supplied by the Metropolitan Police shortly after 9:00am, a time agreed with the manager. She was there to greet the detectives with a stony expression on her face and led them into her office where she gestured for them to take a seat.

'I have to say once again that I am not happy with this, Sergeant,' she said. 'And was it really necessary to have a patrol car parked outside the home all night? Things like that can really upset our residents.'

'Needs must,' said Gallagher. He'd had more than enough of her complaints.

'Are you *really* sure that he killed that poor woman?' said the manager. 'You've seen him. He's an old man and very frail.'

'But he wasn't when she died,' said the sergeant. 'We have to follow the evidence, even if we don't like where it takes us. Suffice to say that we have learned things that have roused our suspicions about the professor.'

'And why do you have to take him up north?' said the manager. 'Can you not question him down here? It would be less stressful for him. He's not really up to a three-hundred-mile journey.'

'I am afraid that he has to go,' said Gallagher. He was working hard to retain his equanimity. 'If we end up charging him, he'd have to appear at our local magistrates' court in Levton Bridge.'

'You do realise that he's on a lot of medication, don't you?' said the manager.

'I do, yes, and we are looking at the possibility of him being remanded to a local nursing home if it comes to that.' Noting that she still looked unconvinced, Gallagher decided to take the manager into his confidence. 'Besides, it may be better for his safety if he was not here.'

'Why not?'

'Not to go outside this room,' said Gallagher, 'but the dead woman was the daughter of a criminal family in Glasgow. It's possible that they might want to have their revenge.'

The manager thought for a moment then stood up.

'Come on then,' she said. 'Let's get the whole horrible affair over with. We've packed an overnight bag for him and enough medication to last a couple of weeks. We haven't told him where he's going, as per your request.'

She led them to the professor's room where he was sitting on the bed with his coat on. His overnight bag was by the door.

'Is someone going to tell me what's happening?' he said irritably as they entered the room. He recognised the detectives. 'This isn't still about that young woman, is it?'

'I am afraid it is,' said Gallagher. 'We are taking you up to Levton Bridge for questioning. Do you understand?'

'Of course, I bloody understand, man!' exclaimed the professor. 'I'm not senile. But you're making a big mistake. I had nothing to do with her death.'

'You'll have plenty of chance to state your case in the interview,' replied Gallagher. He glanced at Orr. 'Read him his rights, please, Constable.'

After Orr had done so, she took the old man by the arm to help him to his feet, but he angrily shrugged her off and struggled up on his own before shuffling towards the door, relying heavily on his walking stick, and brushing past the manager and out into the corridor.

* * *

Following confirmation that the professor was on his way north courtesy of a Metropolitan Police car, Jack Harris headed back to Scotland. As he drove the Land Rover to Dumfries and Galloway once more, he stopped on the westbound A75 to walk the dogs. Standing and watching the animals frolic around a couple of fields, the inspector leaned on a gatepost, deep in thought.

The need to inform Davie Grogan that an arrest had been made had provided the inspector with the excuse that he needed to fulfil his promise to John Foster. There were other reasons why Harris wanted to see Grogan again, not least self-preservation. The inspector was acutely aware that he had handled their first encounter poorly and that, even though the Grogans were renowned for resolving their problems without police involvement, devilment could lead them to submit an official complaint. The inspector was acutely aware that such a complaint would give Alan Jay all the ammunition he could ever need to press for his removal from the case and maybe even from the force. The inspector also knew that Philip Curtis's support could only be expected to go so far, and he hoped that a more conciliatory approach to Davie Grogan second time around would eradicate the risk.

There was another reason why Harris wished to return to Scotland. Although he knew that the evidence increasingly pointed to Nesbitt being responsible for Rosie Grogan's murder, it didn't feel to the detective like the case was anywhere near secure. It was all far too circumstantial and he still needed to reassure himself that the Grogans were not involved. Seeing Davie Grogan again felt like the best way to do it.

⁂

With much to occupy his mind, Harris gave a heavy sigh, whistled to the dogs, loaded them into the back of the Land Rover and resumed his journey. This time when he arrived at Davie Grogan's house, he was pleased to see that there were no BMWs parked outside the property. When he pressed the bell, the door was opened by the nurse.

'I'd like to see Davie,' said Harris.

'You can't,' said the nurse.

Harris held up his warrant card.

'This says I can,' he said. 'I know he's ill but I wouldn't be here unless it was important. I'd hate to have to charge you with obstruction.'

The nurse thought for a few moments then reluctantly stood aside to allow him entry to the house.

'You can have ten minutes, no more,' she said. 'Whatever Davie has done in the past, he's a very sick man now, and I'd ask you to remember that the news about the death of his daughter has hit him hard.'

Harris nodded and walked into the living room where he immediately noted that Davie looked much worse than during their previous encounter. His skin was grey and rimed with sweat and his breathing was laboured behind the oxygen mask. That did not stop the fire flashing in the old man's eyes as he viewed the detective with loathing. The nurse stood by the door with a nervous look on her face as she watched her patient, constantly searching his face for signs of stress.

'What the fuck do you want?' asked the old man as the inspector sat down on the sofa.

'I have news for you, Davie. We've arrested someone for Rosie's murder. He's on his way to Levton Bridge to be interviewed.'

Grogan looked surprised.

'Already?' he said. He lowered his oxygen mask so that it was easier to speak. 'Who is it?'

'You don't really expect me to tell you that, do you?' said Harris. 'But I thought you'd like to hear it first from me rather than from the media.'

The old man regarded him suspiciously.

'Is this some kind of sick joke?' he said. 'You had better not have arrested one of the boys. They had nothing to do with Rosie's death. None of us have.'

'It's no joke, Davie. And no, it's neither of the boys. You were right the last time we met. I forgot that you are the victims in all of this and I was out of order.'

'Yes, you were,' said Davie. He gave Harris a look of grudging gratitude. 'Thank you, though. I appreciate it.'

Acutely conscious that he was speaking to a police officer in a way that he had never done before, he quickly resorted to type and glared at Harris.

'But it doesn't change the fact that you accused me and the boys of killing her,' he said. 'That was unforgivable.'

'It was and I apologise. Old habits die hard, I guess.'

'But you're not going to tell me the name of the man you have arrested?'

'You know I can't tell you that, Davie. The last thing I want is your boys running round hell-bent on revenge. Certainly not with Rory so ready to use his knife.'

Grogan thought for a moment.

'He shouldn't have gone for you like that,' he said. 'But he was upset about Rosie. We all were.'

Harris waited for him to add to the comment then gave a slight smile when it was obvious that he was not going to say anything else; clearly, offering an apology to a police officer was a step too far for Davie Grogan.

'What I can tell you,' said the inspector, 'is that the man we have arrested is in his eighties and not from Glasgow.'

'Was he from the college that Rosie went to in London?' asked Grogan.

'And what makes you say that?'

'Angus says that it's the most likely option. Do you know why he killed Rosie?'

'I'll know more after he's been interviewed,' said Harris.

'Is he…?'

'Look, I'm not really supposed to talk about the details of the case.' Harris stood up, overwhelmed with a sudden desire to bring proceedings to an end. In the face of the old man's questions, coming to see Davie Grogan was not feeling like such a good idea. 'I'll keep you informed as best I can.'

The old man nodded, then he donned his oxygen mask, closed his eyes and looked away.

'One more thing,' said Harris. 'My contacts in Glasgow tell me that the boys have been giving John Foster a rough time of it. Well, you can tell them from me that there's no need. I'm the last person he would talk to.'

'But he's an old friend, isn't he?' said Davie Grogan. He opened his eyes and looked keenly at the detective. 'I mean, you can see why we're suspicious, can't you?'

'We may have been friends once but that was a long time ago and our lives have taken different paths. You needn't worry about him.'

'But Angus says that he knew about Meadowview House standing empty,' said Grogan. Despite his frail condition, there was evil in his expression and a glint in his eye. 'Who's to say that he did not kill my Rosie?'

'Goodbye, Davie,' said Harris and left the room.

A few moments later, he found himself walking with a sense of relief out of the house and into the bright morning sunshine. As he did so, Grogan's words reverberated round his mind.

Chapter twenty-one

'Say that again?' exclaimed Gallagher. It was shortly after 4:00pm and, having arrived back in Levton Bridge, he was standing in front of the inspector's desk and staring at his boss in disbelief. 'You've been where?'

'To see Davie Grogan,' repeated Harris.

'And you went on your own?'

Harris nodded.

'You're fucking crazy!' said the sergeant.

Harris looked at him in surprise; even when Gallagher was angry, it was very rare for him to swear.

'And I bet you didn't tell anyone where you were going, did you?' said Gallagher.

'Gillian knew.'

'And she was OK with it, was she?'

'Her reaction was very similar to yours, actually,' said the inspector. 'She thought I should have taken someone with me.'

'I'll bet she did.' Gallagher sat down heavily. 'What if Grogan's sons had been there? Rory and his flashing blade?'

'My sources told me that they were in Glasgow.'

'What if they'd been wrong?' said the sergeant.

'I can handle them,' said Harris.

'You're not Rambo!'

'Why are you so worked up about it anyway?' asked the inspector.

'Because, oddly enough, for all you drive me to distraction sometimes, I do not want to see you come to any harm.' Gallagher shook his head, his anger replaced by concern. 'And sometimes your belief in your abilities borders on the suicidal. It was bad enough for Rory to pull a knife with both of us there but to run the risk of facing it alone? That's madness.'

Harris thought for a few moments; the sergeant's anger had made a big impact on him.

'You're right,' he said. 'I'll be more careful in future.'

'That'll be the day,' said Gallagher. 'And make sure you write a full note of your conversation.'

'You sound like Curtis.'

'And with good cause,' said Gallagher. 'My mate at Roxham Nick says that someone overheard Alan Jay talking about carrying out some sort of review of paperwork.'

'Probably looking for paper clips.'

'This is no laughing matter,' said Gallagher. 'You know what he's like. Why did you go to see Davie, anyway?'

'I needed to get a few things straight in my head. Look him in the eye without the boys being there.'

'And now you've done it, what do you think?'

'That the professor still seems our best option,' said Harris. 'Is he ready to be interviewed?'

Before Gallagher could reply, the sergeant's mobile phone rang and he excused himself and went into the corridor to take the call. As he did so, the inspector's own mobile rang. It was Jenny Armannsson, calling from her office in the Economic Crime Unit at Greater Manchester Police. Harris smiled and took the call.

'Now then,' he said. 'What can I do for you?'

'I heard on the radio that you've arrested someone for your murder?'

'That's right. The former director of the place in London where Rosie was a student. If it had been up to me, I wouldn't have told the media until we were sure, but headquarters wanted to do something to take the pressure off. I'm glad you've rung, I was going to get in touch anyway when I got a moment. The guy we've arrested for the murder was the one who told Geoffrey Haynes about Meadowview House.'

'That makes sense. In fact, I'm ringing about Haynes. Three of the seven cases we've tracked down that look like they're down to him are in London. Oh, and we think we may know his real name.'

'How come?'

'One of his scams was persuading a charity in Tottenham that a house they were planning to turn into a children's home had been left to him by his grandmother,' said Armannsson. 'It's why he keeps trying it on. The people running the charity were more gullible than some of the others and agreed to pay him £15,000 in return for him dropping his claim.'

'Silly people,' said Harris.

'Indeed. Anyway, the money went into a bank account in the name of Edward Goodwill. By the time the trustees realised their mistake, he'd moved it and closed down the account. We think that's his real name, though, because it appears on several other accounts linked to him. You any nearer to tracking him down?'

'Not yet but we will,' said Harris. 'I'm happy for you to handle the interview when we do. We have enough to do with the murder.'

'That's much appreciated. We've had a lean couple of months and a good collar will do a lot to keep the Brass off my back. I'll keep you posted.'

With the call ended, a considerably more cheerful Jack Harris had just started checking his emails on the desktop computer when Gallagher returned to the office. He also looked cheerful as he sat down.

'Some good news, I take it?' said Harris.

'Yeah. That was my mate in the Met. They've tracked down Geoffrey Haynes. The reason his vehicle had not turned up on ANPR is that it's been sitting on the forecourt of a second-hand car dealer in Camberwell but someone took it for a test drive earlier today and it pinged on a camera. The local cops talked to the dealer, who recognised the description of Haynes and gave them the registration of the car he's driving now – and that vehicle has just been clocked heading for the M25. The Met would like to know if you want it pulling over?'

'Yes, please,' said Harris. 'I've had enough of his fun and games. Thank your mate, will you? That's smart work.'

'Yes, will do.' Gallagher's face had assumed a self-satisfied expression. 'But that's not all, we think we know Haynes' real name.'

'That'll be Edward Goodwill, I imagine,' said Harris, returning to his emails and trying to sound as casual as possible.

Gallagher stared at him in amazement.

'How the...?' he said.

Harris looked up from the computer screen.

'I know everything,' he said with a slight smile. 'Worth remembering that, Matty lad.'

'You're no fun anymore,' said Gallagher.

* * *

Edward Goodwill had just exited a roundabout on the outskirts of London when a police patrol car appeared in his rear-view mirror. Its driver flicked on the blues and twos and flashed his headlights. A sick feeling forming in the pit of his stomach told Goodwill that his great adventure was at an end.

Chapter twenty-two

The interview with Professor Nesbitt at Levton Bridge Police Station started badly when Harris and Gallagher discovered the identity of the duty defence solicitor who had been given the task of representing him. A cheerless, sallow-faced man, Gregory Mortimer had little affection for the police and particularly disliked Jack Harris, whose methods he disapproved of. Mortimer's first move was to insist that the interview be halted before it had even started so that the duty doctor could examine the professor. Once the doctor had ruled that Nesbitt was fit to be interviewed, proceedings resumed shortly after 5:30pm.

'I do feel,' said Mortimer, 'that, notwithstanding what your doctor says, it behoves me to remind you once again that my client is very frail.'

'That may be so,' said Harris. 'But he wasn't when Rosie Grogan was murdered, was he?'

'Yes, but he is now,' said the solicitor. 'Indeed, there is a strong argument that this interview should not even be taking place after he has endured such a long journey. Professor Nesbitt is an elderly man, after all.'

'It's a Nazis thing,' said Harris blandly.

The lawyer gave him a sharp look.

'What on earth does that mean?' he asked.

'Just something the CPS lawyer said,' replied Harris. 'That however old someone is, they should still be accountable for their actions.'

'Yes, well, I warn you that at the first sign of your customary heavy-handed tactics, I will be bringing proceedings to a halt and submitting a formal complaint to your commander.'

'I just want to get to the truth,' said Harris. He looked at the professor, who was sitting with hunched shoulders and closed eyes. 'And I don't like people lying to us, which is what your client has done regarding his visits to Meadowview House.'

'Go on then, ask your questions,' said Mortimer. 'The sooner this is over, the sooner he can be returned to London. God knows why you had to drag him all the way up here.'

'Professor,' said Harris, ignoring the solicitor's comment. 'Is it true that you used to bring young female students to this area on unauthorised trips?'

'I certainly did not!' Nesbitt had opened his eyes and his voice was strong and laced with conviction. 'I've already told your sergeant that it would have been against the rules of the Institute.'

'Are you sure you didn't do it anyway?' asked Harris.

'My client has already told you that he didn't,' said the solicitor tartly. 'And if you are simply going to go round and round in circles asking the same question, I fail to see what that would possibly be achieved.'

Harris reached down by the side of his chair and produced a brown A4 envelope, which he placed on the desk and from which he withdrew a single sheet of paper.

'What's that?' asked Mortimer.

'This,' said Harris, holding the document up so that the lawyer could see the scrawled handwriting, 'is a statement from someone who worked at the Henderson Institute of Botany at the same time as Professor Nesbitt.'

Nesbitt looked worried.

'And what does it say?' asked Mortimer.

'That your client is lying through his teeth,' replied Harris.

'Specifically,' said Gallagher, speaking for the first time in the interview, 'that he was on a final warning for taking pretty young students on trips. We believe that Rosie Grogan was one of them.'

Harris reached down again and produced the photograph of Rosie standing on the hillside behind Meadowview House. He placed it on the table.

'We suspect that this picture of Rosie may have been taken by Professor Nesbitt during a visit to the house,' said Harris. The inspector fixed Nesbitt with a hard look which drained the colour from the old man's cheeks. 'Is that true? And if it is true, how come you said it wasn't?'

Mortimer looked with concern at his client, who had closed his eyes again and whose brow now glistened with beads of sweat.

'I think that we should call a halt in proceedings,' said the solicitor.

'You were the one who wanted things over and done with quickly,' said Harris. 'This is your client's opportunity to make that happen. All he has to do is tell the truth.'

'May I at least take a moment alone with him?' asked the lawyer. His demeanour had changed. He had become less confrontational.

'Surely,' said Harris.

The detectives walked into the corridor where Gallagher looked triumphantly at his boss.

'We've got him,' he said.

'Maybe.'

'What do you mean, maybe? You saw how he reacted when you produced Ronson's statement. He was shocked to the core. I reckon he thought that because it was so long ago, we'd not be able to track anyone down who could disprove his story.'

'Let's see what he comes up with before we jump to conclusions,' said Harris. 'If he continues to deny it, we'll have all on proving guilt. He could still walk away from this.'

They stood in silence for several minutes until the interview room door opened and Mortimer appeared.

'My client wishes to make a statement,' he said.

The detectives re-entered the room.

'My client has not told you the entire truth,' said the solicitor as the officers took their seats.

'Well, I'll go to the foot of our stairs,' said Harris. He reached over to switch on the recording machine. 'Go on then, Professor, tell us what really happened.'

'I *did* take students on field trips,' said Nesbitt. 'You are right about that. And you are right that I was on a final warning from the Institute for breaching its rules.'

'Was Rosie Grogan one of the students?' asked Harris. 'And did you take her to Meadowview House?'

'Yes.'

Gallagher shot Harris an exultant look.

The inspector tapped the photograph. 'So, can I assume that you took this then?'

'I did, yes, but there's nothing sinister about it. She had just finished her first year and I knew that she was thinking about doing her dissertation on orchids in upland meadows, so I offered to take her to see the ones behind Old Man Stillwell's house. They are particularly fine.'

'How did you get there?' asked Harris.

'Rosie caught the train from Glasgow and I drove up from London and met her at Roxham Station. We booked into a B&B.'

'Separate rooms?' asked Gallagher.

'Of course!' said Nesbitt. The suggestion that it could be anything else seemed genuinely to have upset him.

'And you didn't try to do anything inappropriate with her?' asked the sergeant.

'Of course not! I don't know what kind of a man you think I am, but it was all above board. Why on earth would you think otherwise?'

'Because several women have told us that they felt uncomfortable in your presence.'

'Well, I have never done anything to warrant such a suggestion,' said Nesbitt. 'Our visit to Meadowview House was entirely scientific.'

'Did George know that you were going to visit him?' asked Harris.

'I thought it best not to tell him. I knew what he was like and thought that we would have more chance of getting to see the meadows if we just turned up. He wasn't very happy at first, but he seemed to take a shine to Rosie. He didn't let us go into the house, but he did agree to take us up the hill. We had a most agreeable couple of hours.'

'What happened after you left?' asked Harris.

'We spent the rest of the day exploring the area, went back to the B&B and went our separate ways the next morning. That's all there was to it.'

'Are you sure that you didn't take Rosie back a second time?' asked Harris. 'After George had died?'

'If she did go back, it wasn't with me,' said the professor.

'So, what did you think when she disappeared?' asked Gallagher.

'I was very disappointed, of course. She was a very keen student, but I knew that her father disapproved of what she was doing so I assumed that he had refused to help her with the costs. The grants did not cover everything and most of the students tended to require some parental assistance with money. From what Rosie said, her father sounded like the kind of man you did not argue with. Anyway, you wanted the truth, well that's it. It was all very innocent.'

'It sounds to me,' said the solicitor, 'that my client has no case to answer when it comes to the murder of this poor young woman.'

'Maybe,' said Harris.

The detectives went into the corridor to discuss their next move, leaving the professor and the lawyer in the interview room.

'I'm sorry, Matty lad,' said Harris. 'I thought you were onto something, I really did, but I'm not buying Nesbitt as the one who killed Rosie. We don't have a shred of evidence against him and it just doesn't feel right.'

'I'm afraid I have to agree,' admitted Gallagher gloomily. 'It's too big a leap from creepy to murderer. Someone else took her to Meadowview House that second time. What do you want to do with him?'

'Release him under investigation and get him back to London.' Harris glanced at his watch. 'It's getting on now, so it'll have to be tomorrow. Can you sort him out with an overnight stay?'

'Already in hand.'

'Excellent,' said Harris. 'I'll ask the Press Office to put something out about him being released first thing tomorrow. Hopefully, when the Grogans hear about it, they'll stop looking for him but maybe your mate in the Met can organise someone to keep an eye on the home for a day or two?'

'I'll ask,' said Gallagher. He sighed. 'Alan Jay will be delighted that John Foster wasn't much use after all that and that we're back to square one.'

'Maybe we're not back to square one,' said Harris.

'What does that mean?'

'Just something Davie Grogan said,' replied the inspector. 'Can't seem to get it out of my head. But if it turns out to be true, it'll make Alan Jay's year, I'm afraid.'

Chapter twenty-three

The force's update about the release of the man being held in connection with the murder was issued shortly before 7:30am the next morning and was widely reported on news channels, which led to numerous calls to the Press Office from journalists wanting to know what was going to happen next. Sitting at his desk and staring gloomily into the middle distance, Jack Harris wished that he could be sure of the answer. He particularly wished that he could dismiss his growing suspicions about John Foster, suspicions that he was, for the moment, keeping to himself. The inspector looked up hopefully as Gallagher walked into the office shortly after 9:00am.

'Don't tell me,' he said. 'Someone has heard that we've released the professor and rung up to confess?'

Gallagher shook his head and slumped into the chair.

'Chance would be a fine thing,' he said. 'No, I came to tell you that Alan Jay has just arrived.'

'The vulture circling the corpse,' said Harris.

'Very prosaic,' replied Gallagher.

Harris's mobile phone rang. He leaned over to look at the readout on the device, which was lying on the table.

The inspector did not recognise the number but he took the call anyway.

'DCI Harris,' he said.

'Hawk, it's John.' Foster sounded anxious. 'I have to see you urgently.'

'Why?'

'I'd rather do it face to face, but I don't want to come to the police station again. I might be seen.'

'Sounds sensible,' said Harris. 'There's a load of journalists out the front.'

'It's not journalists I'm worried about.'

'Then who?' asked Harris.

'I'll explain when we meet. You know the wood near Asterby where we used to watch the badgers when we were kids? I'll meet you there in an hour. Come in an unmarked vehicle, not the Land Rover. You don't want to attract attention to yourself. Oh, and come alone.'

Before Harris could reply, Foster ended the call.

Gallagher noted the troubled expression on the inspector's face.

'Problem?' he asked.

'It's always a problem,' said the inspector. He slipped the phone into his jacket pocket, stood up and reached for his coat. 'That was John Foster. He wants to see me.'

Gallagher also stood up.

'You want some company?' he asked.

'He said to come alone.'

'And when did you ever do as you were told? Besides, I don't think going alone is a good idea, do you?'

'It'll be fine,' said Harris.

'I really think that you need someone with you,' said the sergeant. 'As protection if for no other reason. Given all this professional standards stuff flying about, you can't afford to meet him alone.'

The inspector made as if to brush past Gallagher but the sergeant blocked his way. For a few moments, they stood toe to toe, the sergeant's pulse racing as he confronted his boss in a way like never before. He'd seen Harris drop men for less. However, it was Harris who backed down and returned to his seat. Gallagher breathed a sigh of relief, sat down and took a few moments to select the right words.

'I know you don't want to hear this,' he said, 'but you don't seem to be giving enough credence to the possibility that it was John who killed Rosie. After all, he was in Glasgow around the time that she vanished, wasn't he?'

Gallagher looked with trepidation at the inspector but Harris remained calm.

'Go on,' he said.

'Well, we know that he knocked around with the Grogans,' said the sergeant. 'Maybe he met Rosie. Maybe he even had a thing for her. He'd have been old enough to drive, maybe it was him who took her back to Meadowview House and she persuaded him to keep it a secret from Davie and the boys. Maybe something happened there, pretty girl, young lad with raging hormones. He'd know that the body was unlikely to be found for a long time so maybe he left it there. Maybe he's sat on the secret for thirty years.'

'You've thought it through, haven't you?' said Harris. 'However, yet again you underestimate me. For your information, from the moment I discovered that John had a relationship with the Grogans, I was thinking along the same lines.'

'So why not tell me?' exclaimed Gallagher, unable to conceal his exasperation. 'Instead of letting me get all excited about the professor?'

'Because until we interviewed Nesbitt, I thought that he was our best suspect.'

'Well, if it does turn out to be Foster, Alan Jay will have your badge.'

Harris stood up again.

'Let's find out what we're dealing with first, shall we?' he said.

'Are you going to let me go with you?'

Harris eyed the sergeant's earnest expression for a few moments then held up his hands in surrender.

'OK, OK, you can come,' he said. He gave Gallagher a rueful look. 'If only to stop you talking. Not that it's ever worked before.'

* * *

Having left the dogs in the CID room, the two men travelled in Gallagher's car to a spot several miles beyond Asterby village in the heart of the valley. The sergeant parked on the track leading up the hillside towards the wood and, having satisfied themselves that the vehicle could not be seen from the road, the detectives walked towards the trees. As they approached the edge of the wood, John Foster stepped into view and scowled when he saw Gallagher. He gave Harris an accusing look.

'I said come alone,' he said.

'I know you did,' said Harris. 'But you can trust Matty and, frankly, the way things have been going, I'm not sure I can trust you. You're too tied up with the Grogans for that.'

'It's a fair enough point, I suppose,' said Foster. He took a nervous look down the slope. 'Were you followed?'

'No,' said Harris. 'Look, what's all this cloak and dagger stuff about, John?'

Foster led the way into the wood and, once the trees had concealed them from the road, turned to look at the detectives with a troubled look on his face.

'Things are getting heavy,' he said. 'Angus saw the piece on Sky News saying that you had released the guy you arrested and he wants me to go back to Glasgow. I rang a couple of my mates and they say that he has got it into his head that it must have been me who killed Rosie because I knew about the house.'

Harris looked intently at his old friend.

'And is he right?' he asked softly. 'Did you kill Rosie?'

'Of course I didn't.' Foster looked hurt at the suggestion. 'And I'm disappointed that you could even think it of me. After all the years we've known each other.'

'I haven't seen you for thirty years. Besides, the job dictates that I think the worst of everyone.' Harris glanced at Gallagher. 'It's a lesson about which I have, quite rightly, been reminded this morning.'

'Well, I didn't kill her,' said Foster. He was battling strong emotions now and his eyes glistened with tears. 'I would never do something like that to Rosie. I cared too much for her to do that. You must believe that.'

'I'll only believe it if you tell me everything,' said Harris.

Foster glanced over towards a series of excavations in the soil nearby.

'The badger sett's still there,' he said with a smile. 'It's still lived in after all these years. Same family of badgers, I imagine. They were good days, weren't they, Hawk? Less complicated.'

'Complicated's the word,' said Harris.

The tears finally began to flow down Foster's cheeks and the detectives gave him time to recover his composure. After a few moments, he wiped his eyes with a handkerchief.

'I couldn't tell you before because it looked bad for me,' he said eventually. 'But I worshipped that woman. Absolutely worshipped the ground she walked on. Trouble was, she could have had her pick of anyone and I was just some kid from the sticks with acne and a painful case of shyness. I don't think she knew that I even existed.'

The detectives smiled as they remembered their own teenage years.

'Then one day, it all changed,' said Foster. 'We got talking and I told her where I was from. She told me about Meadowview House and was amazed when I said that I knew it well. I think she welcomed the opportunity to talk to someone about botany without being shot down. She said she'd been to the house once – she wouldn't tell me who with – and planned to return. I had just got my first car and offered to take her. She agreed but said that I was not to tell Davie or the boys because it would make them mad and she was worried about what they might do.'

'But you were still prepared to risk it?' said Harris.

'You've seen her picture,' said Foster. 'Wouldn't you? I tell you, I felt ten feet tall.'

'So did you take her?'

'It never happened,' said Foster sadly. 'Before we were able to fix something up, she vanished. Angus said she had been kidnapped by a rival gang.'

'And did you believe him?' asked Harris.

'I was just some snot-nosed kid. Who was I to disagree with someone like Angus Grogan? Besides, it seemed plausible. There was a lot of crazy stuff happening at the time. And the police were saying the same thing. As the years went by, people stopped mentioning her. It seemed that Rosie was forgotten.'

'But you didn't forget her, did you?' said Harris.

The tears started once more in Foster's eyes as he shook his head.

'I tried to,' he said. 'Got married, had kids, but I never stopped thinking of poor Rosie. Then her remains turned up at Meadowview House and, like I said the last time we met, 1 got to thinking that perhaps she did go there with one of her lecturers, after all.'

'Did you tell Angus what you suspected?'

'There was no way I was going to get involved,' said Foster. 'Besides, he'd worked it out for himself.'

'And now that we've ruled that out as a possibility, who do you think killed her?' asked Harris.

'I don't know for definite.' The reply came across as evasive and Foster had looked away from them.

'I think you believe that it was one of the Grogans,' said Harris. 'Am I right?'

'They would kill me if they thought I'd told you that. Besides, I was wrong about the lecturer, wasn't I?'

'You were, but I think that you're right about the Grogans,' said Harris. 'I allowed myself to lose sight of it because people kept telling me that they were the victims. People like that are never the victims. Would you be prepared to help us? We'll arrange protection for you and your family.'

'Help you how?' said Foster suspiciously.

'We need to find out which one of them did it. All I need you to do is refuse to go back to Glasgow and let the Grogans know where you are.'

'What!'

'We have to flush them out, John. Force them into making a mistake.'

'Killing me is one hell of a mistake!' Foster watched in alarm as Harris took his mobile phone out of his coat pocket. 'What are you going to do?'

'What I should have done a long time ago,' said Harris. He called up contacts and hit the button for Detective Sergeant Graham Leonard in the Glasgow Organised Crime Unit. 'Graham. Jack Harris. How do you fancy making up for being rude to Alison Butterfield?'

Chapter twenty-four

Daylight had long since faded over the northern hills as the car's headlights picked their way along the valley road in the direction of Carpbery and the cottage where John Foster had grown up. Alistair Marshall and Sally Orr watched the vehicle pass as they sat in their car, which was parked down a farm track. Orr felt a thrill as she saw the driver hunched over the steering wheel, his face silhouetted in the dim light thrown up by the dashboard. She reached for the radio and called Harris, who was waiting with Gallagher and Foster in the living room at the cottage.

'We've just seen the car,' she said. 'It looked like Rory driving.'

'Is he on his own?' asked the inspector.

'Seems to be.'

A couple of minutes later, another set of headlights appeared, also heading towards Carpbery, and the radio crackled into life once more and the voice of Graham Leonard came over the airwaves.

'I think he's nearly there,' said the Glasgow detective. 'Although fuck knows where there is. Give me Glasgow, any day.'

145

'See you soon,' said Harris.

He and Gallagher had been sitting in the living room for the best part of two hours, having left Levton Bridge Police Station when the Glasgow surveillance team had confirmed that Grogan was on his way. Foster, who had been growing increasingly uneasy as the radio updates charted the gangster's progress, glanced at Harris, whose features were impassive. Gallagher, for his part, tried not to look nervous in front of his boss but could feel his heart pounding and his palms were sweaty. He was not relishing another encounter with Rory Grogan.

'I hope you know what you're doing, Hawk,' said Foster.

'Don't worry,' said Harris. 'I told you, I've got officers all over the village and a firearms team parked up behind the church. What's the worst thing that can happen?'

'Rory Grogan kills me.'

'There is that.' Harris gave a low chuckle.

'It's not funny,' protested Foster.

'Relax, will you? Besides, even if he does go for you, you've got that stab-proof vest on under your jumper, haven't you? Not that he'll get anywhere near you because I'll stop him.'

'Yes, well it still sounds risky.'

'Like I said, we have to catch him in the act to get a charge to stick.'

'Why does none of that reassure me?' said Foster.

'You worry too much,' said Harris.

'And you don't worry enough,' said Foster.

'I've been telling him that as long as I've known him,' said Gallagher.

The radio crackled again.

'Ballard here,' said the Glasgow detective, who was travelling with Leonard. 'He's almost at the village.'

'Thank you,' said Harris. 'Stand by, everybody.'

Grogan's vehicle entered Carpbery and drew to a halt alongside the green where Rory cut the headlights, turned off the engine and got out. He looked around uneasily. A city man born and bred, this world was alien to him and he found himself unnerved by the darkness and the silence. He took a scrap of paper out of his back pocket and read it using the light cast by his mobile phone then peered into the darkness and started to make his way tentatively towards a row of terraced houses.

From their hiding place behind the brick-built bus shelter on the far side of the green, Gillian Roberts and Alison Butterfield heard his footsteps as he crossed the grass. They tried not to make a sound as he passed by, so close that they could hear his breathing. Rory stopped at the bottom of the street and flashed his light onto the road sign. Satisfied that he had the right place, he walked slowly up to where the terraced houses gave way to several detached cottages.

Grogan stopped outside the final property on the road, checked the number against his piece of paper and paused with his hand on the front gate as he peered into the darkness, seeking sign of movement through the curtains at the window of the dimly lit living room. Seeing nothing, he pushed open the gate, wincing as it squeaked slightly, and walked up the drive. Finding the front door open, he stepped into the hallway, standing in the darkness for a few moments, straining to hear any sounds and growing ever more uneasy.

Outside, the firearms team started to move slowly through the shadows in the direction of the cottage. Roberts and Butterfield watched them pass by the bus shelter then their attention was diverted by the arrival of another car which cut its headlights and parked on the far side of the green.

'Our Glasgow friends,' said Roberts.

Butterfield did not reply; her pride was still smarting from the way Leonard and Ballard had treated her in the service station and she did not relish meeting them again.

Back in the cottage, Grogan took another step into the darkness.

'John!' he shouted. 'It's pointless hiding. I know you're here!'

Harris glanced at Foster and nodded. As the inspector and Gallagher moved quietly into the adjoining kitchen, Foster stood up and switched on a table lamp.

'In here!' he shouted.

Rory Grogan saw the light, relaxed slightly, produced his knife from his jacket pocket and walked up to the door into the living room. He hesitated for a few moments to ensure that there was nothing to fear then pushed his way into the room where his eyes alighted on Foster. Grogan gave a leer.

'You should have run when you had the chance,' he said. He looked round the room for a few moments. 'Are we alone? Where's your mother?'

'She's gone to stay with a friend,' said Foster. 'I thought it best.'

Grogan gave a wicked smile and the blade of the knife glinted in the firelight as he held up the weapon so that Foster could see it.

'I'll dare say it is,' said Grogan. He ran a finger lightly along the blade, smiling as pinpricks of blood appeared on his flesh. 'I'd hate her to see what I'm going to do to you for killing Rosie.'

'But I didn't kill her.'

'Don't play games with me,' said Grogan. 'I know that you did it.'

'But I didn't,' repeated Foster. 'Who told you I did?'

'Angus,' said Grogan. 'He said that it had to be you and that before I kill you, I have to get you to confess it.'

His voiced tailed off as he watched in horror as the door to the kitchen swung slowly open and Harris and Gallagher appeared.

'What the…?' he exclaimed.

'John has got nothing to confess,' said Harris, stepping into the living room. In that moment, he knew who had killed Rosie Grogan. 'Angus has set you up.'

Grogan stared in dumbstruck silence at the detectives then whirled round to glare furiously at Foster.

'You bastard!' he snarled. His grip tightened round the handle of the knife.

'Put the knife down, Rory,' said Harris calmly. 'Before you do something that we'll both regret. You're going away for a long enough stretch as it is. You could get life for attempted murder. Angus will get the same when we charge him with murder.'

'Murdering who?' asked Grogan. His bewilderment was clear.

'Your sister.'

'Don't talk shite! Angus didn't kill her.' Grogan pointed the knife at Foster. 'He did.'

'Think about it,' said Harris. 'Who's the one who kept coming up with suspects to turn attention away from himself? When Rosie disappeared, who was the one who came up with a cock and bull story about another gang kidnapping her? Then when that proved to be wrong, who said that it must be someone from the college? And when that turned out not be the case, who suggested that it was down to John and sent you to kill him so no one could prove otherwise? Face it, Rory, your brother has thrown you under the bus.'

'He wouldn't do that,' said Grogan. However, he sounded less sure of himself.

'I think he would. I think he did.' Harris stretched out a hand. 'Give me the knife before you do something stupid. You can't get away, the house is surrounded by cops and some of them are armed.'

Grogan hesitated then gave an enraged roar and lunged at Foster with the knife raised but Harris was too quick for him and moved to block the blow. The inspector gave a cry of pain as the blade sliced into his wrist, sending blood spurting onto the carpet. Harris doubled up, clutching his arm. Grogan stared at him for a moment, as if unable to believe what he had done, and Foster seized his opportunity and ran into the hallway. Grogan brandished the knife at a horrified Gallagher, who stared at his wounded boss then took a step forward.

'Don't be a hero!' exclaimed Grogan. He looked down at Harris. 'Not unless you want to end up like him.'

Gallagher stopped.

'Now, get out of the way,' said Grogan.

He gestured with the knife for the sergeant to stand back then stepped over Harris's hunched figure and moved towards the kitchen, where he turned and caught sight of Foster framed in the doorway to the hall. Grogan gave him a menacing look.

'I'll get you for this, one day, you bastard,' he snarled.

He disappeared into the kitchen where he wrenched open the door and ran out into the back garden. Gallagher moved to attend to Harris, who was still on his knees, clutching his wrist. His face was pale and his features were twisted in pain.

'Are you alright?' gasped Gallagher.

'Do I look alright?' said Harris through gritted teeth. 'But forget about me. Don't let him get away.'

Gallagher hesitated.

'Go!' exclaimed Harris.

The sergeant heard the clatter of Grogan colliding with a dustbin in the garden and ran out of the house in time to see him hurdle the back fence and disappear into the darkness. Back at the green, the armed officers were edging their way up the street when they saw the shape of a fleeing man in the shadows.

'Don't shoot!' cried the senior officer. 'Not until we're sure it's him!'

The officer's voice brought forth a cry of alarm from Grogan and he sprinted across the green towards his car. Seeing that two uniformed officers were standing by it, he gave a bellow of frustration and veered towards Graham Leonard and Mary Ballard, who were standing next to their vehicle. They reacted too slowly and Grogan grabbed Ballard, holding the knife to her throat. As the armed officers approached, he held her tighter and she squealed in terror as she felt the blade on her flesh.

'One step nearer and I'll kill her!' he shouted. 'Drop your weapons!'

The armed officers hesitated but another squeal from Ballard made up their minds and they did as instructed. Grogan pointed to Leonard.

'You,' he said. 'Drive.'

He wrenched open the car's rear door and bundled Ballard onto the back seat then noticed that Leonard was still standing outside the vehicle. Grogan brandished the knife at the detective again.

'I said fucking drive,' he snarled.

Before the Glasgow detective could react, a figure loomed out of the darkness, moving at pace, and slammed into a startled Grogan, knocking him against the side of the vehicle, driving the air from his lungs and sending the knife spiralling through the air to clatter harmlessly onto the nearby road. Grogan gave a cry of pain as Alison Butterfield twisted his arms behind his back and snapped on the handcuffs then dragged him to his feet and gave Leonard a triumphant look.

'And that,' she said, 'is how we do things in the sticks!'

Leonard looked at her glumly and a shaken Mary Ballard got out of the car, rubbed her throat and glanced ruefully at the young detective constable.

'I owe you one,' she said weakly.

'Just chalk it down to experience,' said Butterfield.

Gillian Roberts laughed. All eyes turned to the sight of Gallagher helping Jack Harris across the green, the inspector still looking pale and clutching his wrist, around which was wrapped the sergeant's handkerchief.

'I keep telling him he'll push it too far one day,' said Gallagher, 'but will he listen, will he hell as like?'

Chapter twenty-five

The buzz of excitement in Levton Bridge Police Station later that evening was in sharp contrast to the oppressive silence of the interview room where Harris, the gash on his wrist now heavily bandaged, sat next to Gallagher and looked across the desk at the defiant figure of Rory Grogan, who was next to the duty solicitor. The sergeant cast occasional concerned looks at his boss, who had declined the opportunity to go home and rest.

'Come on, Rory,' said Harris wearily. 'Surely, you realise that the game's up?'

'I'm saying nothing,' replied Grogan. He crossed his arms. 'And you can't make me.'

'I don't really need to,' said Harris. He looked at the solicitor. 'I take it you have told your client that we already have enough witness statements to charge him with numerous offences?'

Harris winced as a jag of pain shot up his wrist.

'Not least attacking me?' he said.

'I have, yes,' replied the lawyer. 'But if he does not wish to talk to you, Chief Inspector, there's nothing I can do.'

'Come on, Rory,' said Harris. 'Time to face facts. You're going away for a long time. As is your brother.'

'You're wrong about him killing Rosie.'

Harris shook his head.

'I think not,' he said.

'He wouldn't do a thing like that,' said Grogan. 'He loved her. We all did. She was our sister, for God's sake.'

'Maybe she was but I think that she was also an inconvenience. Someone who was doing damage to your tough-guy image. I don't think that your brother was prepared to let that happen. It's bad for business.'

'It sounds to me like nothing more than guesswork,' said the solicitor. 'From what I have heard, no court in the land will believe that he killed his sister. You don't seem to have much in the way of evidence.'

'Then we'll get him on accessory to murder,' said Harris. 'It's clear from what Rory said in the cottage that Angus set up the attack on John Foster.'

'I'll deny saying anything,' said Grogan. 'I'm not dropping Angus in it.'

'Even though he set you up?' said Harris.

'I don't believe that he did.'

'It doesn't matter what you believe. He's already texted your mobile three times, asking if you've "done it". I reckon the CPS will think that's enough to prove accessory. Anyway, you should be worrying about yourself.' Harris stood up and headed for the door. 'I suggest that you and your solicitor have a little chat. See if you decide to co-operate.'

Harris and Gallagher left the room, shutting the door behind them.

'The solicitor's right, you know,' said the sergeant when they were in the corridor. 'We've got absolutely nothing to link Angus to the murder.'

'But he doesn't know that, does he?' said Harris. 'I want to see what he does when he finds out what's happened. If he makes a run for it, that would look like the action of a guilty man and we can use that.'

'And if he doesn't?'

Before Harris could reply, Sally Orr approached them, holding up Rory Grogan's mobile phone.

'Angus has been on again,' she said. 'Left a message wanting to know what's happening.'

'Maybe it's time he found out,' said Harris. 'Let Rory have the phone call he keeps asking for. My guess is that he wants to tip off his brother.'

Harris and Gallagher headed back into the interview room.

'Well?' said Harris. He looked at Grogan. 'You going to play ball?'

'I'm saying nothing,' said Grogan. 'And when can I have my phone call?'

'You can make it from the custody suite while I'm talking to the CPS,' said Harris.

* * *

After taking Grogan to the suite, the detectives headed back to the CID squad room, where they found the dogs asleep by the radiator. CPS lawyer Jane Malham was sitting at one the desks, reading reports from the evening's work. She looked up as Harris entered the room.

'Happy to charge Rory?' asked Harris. He sat down at one of the desks and closed his eyes as his arm continued to throb.

'More than happy,' said Malham. 'We can throw the book at him. Has he said anything about Rosie's murder?'

'Nothing,' said Harris. He opened his eyes and glanced at Gallagher, who was filling up the kettle at the sink in the corner of the room. 'And I don't think he will, do you, Matty lad?'

Gallagher turned round, kettle in hand, and shook his head.

'Don't think so,' he said. 'He seemed genuinely shocked at the suggestion that Angus killed her. God knows how we're going to prove it, assuming you are right. You're really flying a kite on this one.'

There was a sound at the door and they turned to see Alan Jay standing there.

'Oops,' said Gallagher.

Harris gave the sergeant a sharp look then turned to Jay, not giving him the opportunity to speak.

'I'm in no mood for your games,' he growled.

'Too busy playing games of your own, from the sound of it,' said Jay. He glanced at the inspector's bandaged wrist and gave a thin smile. 'However, given that you've taken a dangerous man off the streets and are likely to receive a commendation for saving John Foster's life, it might be regarded as somewhat churlish to make too much of it so I'll bid you good night.'

Gallagher waited until the sound of Jay's footsteps had faded away along the corridor then looked at Harris.

'Wonders will never cease,' he said.

'Not so wondrous,' said Harris. 'More like self-preservation. Like he says, if he moves against me now, he doesn't stand a chance of success. He'd rather wait.'

Sally Orr walked into the room.

'Rory made his call yet?' asked Harris.

'He has,' said the constable. 'Rang his brother, as expected. Rory clammed up when he realised that I was listening, but I got the impression that Angus told him to keep his mouth shut.'

'I'll bet he did,' said Harris.

The inspector's mobile phone rang. He fished the device out of his jacket pocket and took the call, putting it on speaker so that the others could hear.

'Jack,' said a voice they recognised as Graham Leonard. He and Ballard were heading back to Glasgow and the Levton Bridge officers could hear the drone of the car engine in the background. 'I've just had word from our surveillance team. Angus is on the move.'

'In which direction?' asked Harris.

'South out of the city. Moving fast. Heading to see Davie, I guess. Do you want him picking up?'

'No,' said Harris. 'Let him run until we're sure.'

Leonard called back later.

'He's turned off the M74,' he said. 'He's on the Dumfries road. He's definitely on his way to see his father.'

'Presumably so that they can get their stories straight,' said Harris. 'Let him get there. How long will it take?'

'An hour maybe.'

'Keep the house under surveillance until I arrive, will you?'

'But what about your arm?' asked Leonard.

'I'll be fine.' Harris ended the call and looked at Gallagher. 'Looks like we're heading back to Dumfries and Galloway, Matty lad.'

Gallagher gave his boss a worried look.

'I do hope you're not planning to drive,' he said.

Harris gave a slight smile.

'No, I think that this time we deserve to travel in a bit of style, don't you?' he said.

The inspector scrolled down the list of contacts on his mobile phone and selected a number. He spoke into the device. 'We're on.'

Not long later, a helicopter from the National Police Air Service swept low over Levton Bridge and landed on the playing field at the primary school close to the police station. Harris and Gallagher were waiting for it.

Chapter twenty-six

As the helicopter headed west towards Dumfries, Harris allowed his gaze to roam to the hills beyond the town. They were mostly in darkness but there was the occasional pinprick of light on the slopes and he wondered which one of them came from Davie Grogan's home. Gallagher was thinking the same.

'What do you think is happening at the house?' he asked, raising his voice to be heard over the clatter of the rotor blades.

'I'm not sure,' said Harris. 'All I know is that people make mistakes when they are under pressure.'

'Angus does not strike me as the type to make mistakes,' said Gallagher. 'Rory, yes, but he strikes me as more careful.'

'Careful or not, it's our last chance, Matty lad. If it doesn't produce anything, I fear that we'll never be able to charge anyone for Rosie's murder.'

'And you're sure it was Angus, are you?'

'Not one hundred per cent but he's the best option. It had to be one of the Grogans and I don't think it was Rory, even though he's a hothead, and I don't think that Davie would kill his own daughter. That leaves Angus.'

'But how do we prove it?' asked Gallagher.

'Now there's a question,' said Harris. His attention was brought back to the town as the aircraft began to descend towards the rooftops. 'We'll find out soon enough.'

The helicopter landed in a field on the edge of town, where Harris and Gallagher walked towards the police patrol vehicle that was waiting for them by the gate.

'I take it Angus is still there?' Harris asked one of the uniform officers who was standing by the car.

'According to our surveillance team, yes,' said the officer. 'There's a light on in the front bedroom. DS Leonard says that he'll meet you there.'

It did not take the patrol car long to leave the town and reach the turning for The Laurels. The first faint streaks of light had just appeared over the hills as the vehicle made its way towards two cars parked halfway up the track. Graham Leonard got out of one of them and joined the Levton Bridge detectives in the patrol car, which continued on towards the house in silence. Once the car had parked in front of the property, the detectives got out and strode past the BMW towards the house where the front door was opened by the nurse.

'Where are they?' asked Harris.

She motioned to the stairs.

'Front bedroom,' she said. 'Davic is dead.'

Harris stared at her.

'Dead?'

'He had a heart attack after Angus rang to tell him what had happened,' said the nurse. 'He died before he got here.'

Harris gave her a hard look.

'Why didn't you call an ambulance?' he asked.

'Angus said you have a suspicious mind,' said the nurse. She held up the sheet of paper that she was holding. The detectives could see the letters DNR printed in bold black letters. The nurse handed the sheet to the inspector. 'It's the same as the Do Not Resuscitate forms you get in hospitals. Davie filled it out himself a few weeks ago. You can see by the shaky handwriting. Myself and Angus signed it as witnesses. Davie was resuscitated by paramedics twice over the summer and he was adamant that the next time he had an attack that he be allowed to die. You saw what he was like. It was no life for him.'

Harris scanned the sheet but said nothing as he headed towards the stairs, followed by Gallagher and Leonard.

'I made him as comfortable as I could,' said the nurse.

She sounded so forlorn that Gallagher glanced back at her and nodded.

'I'm sure you did your best,' he said.

Once on the landing, Harris pushed his way into the front bedroom. Angus was sitting by the bed and his eyes glistened with tears as he looked down at the dead man, whose shrunken, pain-wracked body was finally at peace.

'You're too late,' said Angus. 'You can't charge him now.'

Harris looked surprised.

'Charge him?' he said. 'With what?'

'Killing Rosie. Rory said you think that I did it but you're wrong.' Angus reached down by the side of the bed and produced a cassette recorder. He gave a slight smile. 'Dad was never into technology. He'd had this for twenty years that I can remember. He used it to record his confession.'

Harris gave him a sceptical look.

'How do I know you didn't persuade him to do it to get you off the hook?' he asked.

Angus looked beyond the inspector as the nurse followed Gallagher and Leonard into the bedroom.

'I said he has a suspicious mind, didn't I?' he said. 'Tell him.'

Harris turned to look at the nurse.

'Tell me what?' he said.

'Davie asked me to make the recording after you came to tell us that you had found Rosie,' she said. 'Only he and

I knew that it existed and he said that it was only to be played if you charged either of the boys with killing her and he was dead. Angus only heard it for the first time tonight.'

Angus pressed the 'play' button and they heard the old man's voice, weak, laboured and punctuated by bouts of coughing but recognisable for all that.

'If you're playing this,' said Davie, 'then I have passed on. If you are listening, Chief Inspector, as I suspect you are, I am beyond your reach now. I am recording this because I do not want you to think that either of the boys killed Rosie. I alone am responsible for her death and I have lived with that terrible secret for thirty years. Angus and Rory, I am deeply sorry for what happened to your sister, but I could not allow us to appear weak. When Rosie told me that she planned to go back to Meadowview House for her studies, in defiance of my wishes, it was the final straw. I pretended that I'd had a change of mind and offered to take her. I told her not to let anyone know what we were planning to do because it would damage my reputation.'

A heavy tension had settled on the room as they listened to his words.

'Once we were at the house,' he said, 'I gave her a final chance to mend her ways, but she refused and I lost control. I've always had a temper, it's where Rory gets his impetuous nature from, and I strangled her. I left her body there because I thought it would not be found for a long time and by the time it was, there would be nothing to connect me with the house.'

There was a pause on the tape and when Davie spoke next, there was a catch in his voice.

'Angus, Rory, many times have I regretted my actions that day but I have learned to live with the guilt. I had planned to take the secret to my grave but once her body was found, I could not let either of you be wrongly arrested for killing her. I know how much you loved your sister.'

He stopped talking and the only sound was a faint hissing on the tape. After a few moments, he started speaking again.

'So now you know the truth,' he said. 'I have done many wicked things in my life but nothing as wicked as my actions that day. I hope that this recording atones in some small way for what I did and that you can forgive me and I can go to my rest with my conscience at least a little eased.'

The recording stopped and the Angus hit the 'off' button.

'He stopped talking then,' said the nurse. 'He was crying and he said that he did not want anyone to hear it.'

'So, you see,' said Angus, looking at Harris. 'I didn't kill her and neither did Rory.'

'Unfortunately, the only word we have for that is from someone who is beyond questioning,' said Harris. He looked down at the old man's frail body. 'Some more sceptical souls than me might say that is rather convenient.'

'They may well say that,' replied Angus with the slightest of smiles. 'But it's all you have, isn't it?'

Harris nodded.

'It is,' he said. 'I guess that your father will have to answer to a higher authority than me.'

'He was never a particularly religious man,' said Angus.

'Actually, I was thinking of the Crown Prosecution Service,' said Harris and left the room.

Chapter twenty-seven

Jane Malham reached over to switch off the tape recorder then looked across her desk at Harris and Gallagher with an approving expression on her face.

'That's it then,' she said. 'You've got Rosie's killer. Well done, gentlemen.'

'Maybe,' said Harris.

It was later that morning and, after grabbing a few hours' sleep, the detectives were back at Levton Bridge Police Station where the doctor had applied fresh dressings on Harris's wound then given up on his attempts to persuade the detective to take the remainder of the day off.

'Maybe?' said Malham. 'You don't believe that he did it then?'

'The governor has got it into his head that Davie made up the confession to stop us arresting Angus for murder,' said Gallagher. 'A final act of rare nobility in a life in which there has been precious little.'

'Is that right?' asked Malham. She looked at Harris.

'Maybe it's the fact that it's a tape,' said the inspector. 'I've sat through many a confession in my time and you can usually work out pretty quickly if they're telling the truth. It's something about the eyes but with a tape recording it's more difficult to judge. However, I'm just not convinced that Davie killed her. He always struck me as someone who clung to the hope that his daughter was still alive.'

'What do think, Matthew?' asked Jane.

'It sounds OK to me,' said the sergeant. 'We've got nothing to suggest that Angus killed his sister whereas the old man knew that he'd be dead long before we got him into a court. It's a good old-fashioned deathbed confession. Clearing the decks before he went to meet his maker.'

'Agreed,' said Malham. She reached for her mug of tea. 'And my boss is happy to accept it as such. From the CPS's point of view, you have a perfectly valid confession and nothing to say otherwise. Unless you're unhappy with the nurse's account of how it was taken? What do we know about her?'

'Nothing to set alarm bells ringing,' said Gallagher. He flicked to a page in his notebook. 'Emma Craven, aged thirty-seven, a divorcee with a thirteen-year-old son who lives with his father. She lives just outside Dumfries. She's one of three nurses provided by an agency.'

'All living in?' asked Harris.

'Yeah, they'd been taking it in turns. Emma was three weeks into her latest stint. I've asked Alison to ring her to see if she wants to add anything to the statement she gave at the house last night but I'm not expecting anything. It all seems very straightforward.'

'And Rory, what's he saying?' asked Malham.

'The same as his brother,' said Harris. 'Shocked that his father killed Rosie.'

'So, is it not possible that Davie was telling the truth?' asked Malham.

'I guess so,' said Harris but he still didn't sound convinced. 'And even if Angus is guilty, there's no way that he's going to admit it. He knows that we've got nothing on him.'

'Well, given that you've got nothing on which we could build a case, you have no alternative but to let him go,' said Malham.

'Can we not at least charge him with accessory on the attempted murder of John Foster?' asked Gallagher. 'He clearly set Rory up.'

'Maybe he did, Matthew, but I can't see us bringing charges unless Rory changes his mind and makes a statement and he's clearly very loyal to his brother. And even if he did say something, it's still pretty thin.'

'What about the texts from Angus asking if he'd done it?' asked the sergeant.

'It might help strengthen a case but it's not enough on its own,' said Malham. 'Don't look so glum, guys, you've got Rory for attempted murder and you know who killed his sister. That sounds like a good result to me.'

Harris nodded, drained his mug of tea and stood up.

'I guess you're right,' he said. 'Much as it pains me, I'll let Angus go.'

The detectives walked out into the corridor where Gallagher headed for the CID squad room and Harris walked back towards the interview room. As he did so, his mobile phone rang. He took the call.

'Ross,' he said. 'I'm a bit tied up at the moment. Can it wait?'

'It's just a quickie,' said the Wildlife Trust director. 'We've been talking at this end and we're touched by the story of Rosie Grogan. We are thinking that we'd like to name the new library at the visitor centre after her in recognition of her determination to study botany. What do you think?'

'I'm not sure I like the idea of glorifying the Grogans, Ross.'

'Yes, but this wouldn't be doing that, would it?' said Makin. 'If anything, it's the opposite and it would be our way of paying tribute to Rosie. We think that it would send out a powerful message. Would you mention it to the family for us?'

'I suppose so,' said Harris. 'If you're sure.'

'We are.'

The inspector ended the call and went back into the interview room where Angus was sitting with his solicitor.

'I've talked to the CPS,' said Harris. He sat down and winced as he banged his wrist against the edge of the table. 'You're free to go.'

'I should think so,' said Grogan. He stood up. 'You seem to have forgotten that I have lost my father, Chief Inspector. Indeed, you consistently seem to forget that we are the victims in all of this. I've half a mind to submit a formal complaint.'

'Don't push it,' growled Harris. He gave him a hard look. 'But be in no doubt that you got lucky this time.'

The lawyer opened his mouth to protest but Angus held up a hand to prevent him speaking.

'Leave it,' he said. 'He really isn't worth it.'

Harris decided not to rise to the bait.

'One thing before you go,' he said instead. 'The Wildlife Trust would like to create a library at Meadowview House and name it in honour of your sister. They asked if that would be alright with you?'

Angus gave a slight smile.

'Dad would have hated the idea,' he said.

'As do I,' said Harris. 'What do *you* think?'

'I guess it would be kind of appropriate,' said Angus. 'After all, she loved reading, did Rosie, and the old fellow's books did keep her company when she was lying in Meadowview House for all those years, didn't they? I can take some solace from that, I suppose. Tell the Wildlife Trust yes.'

'All in good time,' said Harris. He had always contended that if you waited long enough, a guilty person would eventually make the mistake in an unguarded moment that gave them away. He sensed that Angus had done just that. 'But first, perhaps you'd like to tell me how you know about the books in the house?'

'What do you mean?'

'All I said was that the Trust was planning to create a library.' There was an edge to the inspector's voice now. 'Only someone who had been in the house would know that the books were already there.'

'I must have read it somewhere,' said Angus.

'I don't think you did. It hasn't been reported. In fact, the Trust has been keeping the existence of George Stillwell's library a secret until the reopening.'

Angus looked uneasy.

'Then John Foster must have told me,' he said. 'He'd been there. Yes, that must be it.'

'Wait here a minute,' said Harris.

He walked out into the corridor. Back in the interview room, Angus looked increasingly worried. Harris had just finished his call to John Foster when Gallagher approached along the corridor. He looked like a man with news to impart.

'Something happening?' asked Harris.

'The nurse has gone missing. She's not answering her mobile and the agency says that she gave in her notice first thing this morning. Her manager said that she sounded really upset.'

'Upset how?'

'Frightened. I've put out an alert for her car.'

Harris rubbed his hands together.

'It's unravelling, Matty lad,' he said. 'I think that our Miss Craven knows more than she is letting on. Come on, let's give Angus the good news.'

Thirty seconds later, the detectives were back in the interview room and Harris was surveying Angus Grogan with a glint in his eye that Gallagher was later to describe as like a predator eyeing its prey. Grogan looked at him with an increasing sense of anxiety.

'What's happening?' he asked.

'I am afraid that you will be staying with us a little longer than we envisaged,' said Harris. 'If I'm right, thirty years longer.'

'What does that mean?' asked the solicitor.

'It means,' said Harris, 'that I am holding your client on suspicion of murdering his sister.'

* * *

It took just thirty minutes for Emma Craven's car to trigger an ANPR camera as the vehicle approached Prestwick Airport and just a few minutes more for a Police Scotland patrol driver to flick on the blue lights and pull her over.

Chapter twenty-eight

'A somewhat last-minute decision to go on holiday, Miss Craven,' said Harris, looking across the desk at the nurse. 'So last minute that you appear not to have even purchased an air ticket. Perhaps you would care to explain exactly what's been happening at The Laurels?'

It was mid-afternoon and he and Gallagher were talking to Emma Craven in one of the interview rooms at Levton Bridge Police Station, where she had been brought following her apprehension near the airport. She did not reply.

'Well?' said Harris as the silence lengthened. 'We're waiting.'

'I can't,' she said. Her voice was so quiet that the detectives struggled to hear the words. 'I just can't.'

'Then how about telling us where you were going in such a hurry?' asked the inspector.

'Spain.'

'Why?'

'I have a sister who lives in Malaga.'

'And why the rush to see her today of all days?' asked Harris.

Craven shook her head.

'Then let me help you,' said Harris. 'You see, I think you know that Davie's confession was false and I am guessing that you were trying to get away because Angus knows that you know. What did he threaten you with? Harming a member of your family? It's usually something like that in such situations. Am I right?'

Tears started in her eyes and she buried her face in her hands.

'This is a nightmare,' she moaned.

'Yes, and it can only come to an end if you help us get Angus locked up. Who did he threaten?'

She fought back strong emotions for a few moments then appeared to make a decision.

'My son,' she said with a stronger voice. 'He said that he knew where he lived.'

'Well, if you give us your son's address, we can ask our colleagues in Scotland to check that he's OK,' said Harris.

'He'll be at school now,' she said.

'Well, jot the name of the school down and we'll sort it.'

Harris tore a sheet of paper from his notepad and slid it across the table, also furnishing her with a pen. Once she had written down the details, the inspector gave the note to Gallagher and the sergeant left the room to make the necessary arrangements. He returned a few minutes later.

'Officers are on the way to the school,' he said as he took his seat again.

'Your son will taken into protective custody until we can work out how best to proceed,' said Harris.

'Thank you,' said Craven.

'Now for your side of the bargain,' said the inspector. 'Whose idea was it for Davie to make the recording? Angus, I am assuming?'

She nodded.

'After you came to see Davie to tell him that you'd found Rosie's remains,' she said. 'The boys went back to Glasgow after you'd left but Angus came back that evening. He told me to stay outside his father's room but halfway through the recording Davie took a turn for the worst and I had to go to him. That's when I realised what was happening.'

'Did you get the impression that Davie was making the recording willingly?' asked Harris.

'No,' she said. 'He told Angus that he didn't want people to think that he killed his daughter but Angus was very persuasive and said it was the only way to stop you sending him to prison. Davie didn't really have the strength to fight him.'

'And Angus threatened to hurt your son if you told anyone?' said Harris

Craven nodded. She was fighting back the tears.

'That's why I decided to go to Spain,' she said. 'I told Angus that you would not be able to pressure me if I was not in Dumfries.'

'Are you prepared to write a statement about what happened?' asked Harris.

'If you can guarantee that my son will be safe.'

Harris looked at Gallagher as the sergeant's mobile phone pinged as a text arrived.

'They've just picked him up,' he said.

'Then yes,' said Craven. 'No one should get away with threatening a young boy like that.'

A few minutes later, Harris and Gallagher had summoned Angus Grogan from the cells and were back in the interview room. Grogan looked worried and kept glancing at his lawyer.

'Why is my client still here?' asked the solicitor. 'You have nothing to suggest that he killed Rosie.'

'Au contraire,' said Harris. 'You see, we've just had an interesting chat with Emma Craven…'

Grogan closed his eyes. Sitting and surveying his ashen features, Jack Harris was acutely aware of the throbbing pain in his wrist.

Chapter twenty-nine

Jack Harris gave a slight smile as the foreman of the jury at Manchester Crown Court stood up at the end of Edward Goodwill's trial and pronounced the first of the verdicts on the seven deception charges. The aftermath of the Grogan case, plus a myriad of other competing demands, had pushed thought of the con man to the back of the inspector's mind but now he leaned forward eagerly in his seat in the public gallery. Goodwill stood in the dock with his eyes closed at the end of a three-week trial in which he had frequently changed his story and had been rebuked several times by the judge for heckling witnesses. He looked shocked when the first guilty verdict was read out.

Sitting next to Harris, Jenny Armannsson murmured 'yes' under her breath and Gallagher gave a nod of approval at each of the subsequent guilty verdicts. Sitting at the end of the row, Ross Makin had a relieved look on his face. With the official opening of the George Stillwell Visitor Centre due to happen the following week, complete with the unveiling of the Rosie Grogan Natural History Library, the thought of Goodwill being acquitted had been giving the Wildlife Trust director sleepless nights.

There was to be no representative of the Grogan family at the event at Meadowview House. One morning the previous week, Harris and Gallagher had sat in a similar gallery at Carlisle Crown Court to see Angus jailed for life after being found guilty of murder following a week-long trial. In the afternoon, his brother was sent to prison for fourteen years after admitting the attempted murder of John Foster and the assault on Harris. The inspector had been awarded a judge's commendation for his bravery in confronting the knifeman.

'Edward Goodwill,' said the judge. She fixed the prisoner with a hard stare. 'You have been found guilty of a series of heinous crimes related to your efforts to deceive and before I pass sentence, I must commend the police, particularly Detective Inspector Armannsson, for their painstaking work in allowing the jury to fully appreciate the extent of your wicked lies.'

Armannsson smiled and Harris patted her arm appreciatively.

'You have,' continued the judge, 'cynically targeted those more trusting than yourself, threatening worthy projects including those catering for some of the most vulnerable people in our society, and I have no compunction in sending you to prison for six years.'

'Excellent,' said Harris.

Outside the court, the inspector turned on his mobile phone and listened to the message that had been left for him. When he had finished, he slipped the device back into his jacket pocket and looked cheerfully at the others.

'Good news?' asked Gallagher.

'That was Gillian. She thought I'd like to know that a Levton Bridge mother has been in to say that she's found a load of spray paint cans in her son's bedroom and that he has admitted to being our graffiti artist. Rather bizarrely, Boz is actually called Graham. Go figure.'

Before anyone could comment, the inspector's mobile pinged as he received a text. He read it and gave the biggest smile that Gallagher had ever seen him produce.

'It would appear,' said the inspector, 'that Alan Jay has been overlooked for the permanent job at Professional Standards. He's going back to chief inspector and is returning to his old role in the admin department.'

He clapped his hands with delight.

'Still, mustn't grumble, eh?' he said. 'Those paper clips won't count themselves.'

He slipped his arm into Jenny's.

'Now then, Ms Armannsson,' he said. 'Would you care to suggest a bar where we can raise a glass in celebration of today's events? Preferably somewhere outside the city? For some reason, I'm not very popular with some people here. Can't think why.'

THE END

List of characters

Levton Bridge Police:

Superintendent Philip Curtis – divisional commander
Detective Chief Inspector Jack Harris – head of divisional CID
Detective Inspector Gillian Roberts
Detective Sergeant Matthew Gallagher
Detective Constable Alison Butterfield
Detective Constable Alistair Marshall
Detective Constable Sally Orr

County Police Force:

Acting Superintendent Alan Jay

Other police service personnel:

Detective Inspector Jenny Armannsson – Head of the Greater Manchester Police Economic Crime Unit
Detective Constable Mary Ballard – officer in the Glasgow Organised Crime Unit
Detective Sergeant Graham Leonard – officer in the Glasgow Organised Crime Unit

Malcolm Gray – retired Glasgow detective
Sergeant Jamie Ross – Police Scotland firearms officer

The Grogan Family:

Davie – father
Angus – son
Rory – son
Rosie – daughter

Other characters:

Emma Craven – nurse
Hannah Crosby – freelance archivist
John Foster – Glasgow car dealer
Geoffrey Haynes – a Londoner
David Ledbitter – charity chief executive
Betty Lord – pensioner
Gerald Lucas – solicitor
Jane Malham – Crown Prosecution Service lawyer
Ross Makin – director Three Valleys Wildlife Trust
Gregory Mortimer – solicitor
Professor Gordon Nesbitt – retired lecturer
Professor James 'Doc' Rokeby – Home Office pathologist
Gail Ronson – retired college worker
Amanda Scarff – charity chief executive
George Stillwell – former owner of Meadowview House

If you enjoyed this book, please let others know by leaving a quick review on Amazon. Also, if you spot anything untoward in the paperback, get in touch. We strive for the best quality and appreciate reader feedback.

editor@thebookfolks.com

www.thebookfolks.com

ALSO BY JOHN DEAN

In this series:

Dead Hill (Book 1)
The Vixen's Scream (Book 2)
To Die Alone (Book 3)
To Honour the Dead (Book 4)
Thou Shalt Kill (Book 5)
Error of Judgement (Book 6)
The Killing Line (Book 7)
Kill Shot (Book 8)
Last Man Alive (Book 9)

In the DCI John Blizzard series:

The Long Dead
Strange Little Girl
The Railway Man
The Secrets Man
A Breach of Trust
Death List
A Flicker in the Night
The Latch Man
No Age to Die
The Vengeance Man

DISCOVER JOHN DEAN'S DCI JOHN BLIZZARD SERIES

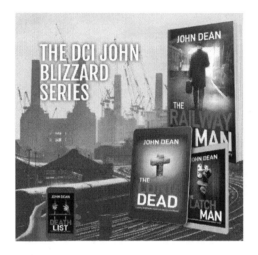

All ten books are FREE with Kindle Unlimited and available in paperback.

www.thebookfolks.com

Made in the USA
Middletown, DE
03 August 2022